HOLDING ON

Richard Snodgrass

Stories of Furnass

 Calling Crow Press

Pittsburgh

Also by Richard Snodgrass

Fiction

There's Something in the Back Yard

The Books of Furnass

All That Will Remain

Across the River

Holding On

Book of Days

The Pattern Maker

Furrow and Slice

The Building

Some Rise

All Fall Down

Redding Up

Books of Photographs and Text

An Uncommon Field: The Flight 93
Temporary Memorial

Kitchen Things: An Album of Vintage Utensils
and Farm-Kitchen Recipes

Memoir

The House with Round Windows

Published by Calling Crow Press
Pittsburgh, Pennsylvania

Book design by Book Design Templates, LLC
Cover Design by Jack Ritchie

Printed in the United States of America
ISBN 978-0-9997699-4-2
Library of Congress catalog control number: 2018911042

Contents

This is Marty's book.

With small town people, every story

is part of some other story.

William Maxwell

1764

The two Highlanders of the Black Watch, the 42nd Royal Highland Regiment of Foot, struggle through the dense thickets up the slope from the river. Hack with their basket-hilted broadswords at the tangles of vines and blood-red leaves. Brambles snag at their dark government-issue kilts, already torn and ragged from years of wear. Thorns catch at the long plaids thrown back over their shoulders, at their scarlet tunics and cartridge pouches and muskets. Still the two men slip and stumble on. On up the stony embankment, grabbing tree trunks and vines and handfuls of grass, using anything they can to help pull themselves up, reaching for anything except each other, on up the hillside into the trees.

In a hundred years there will be a town here, a small community of a few thousand people settled around an iron furnace and a brickyard farther up in the hills, a gristmill and a steamworks and a boatyard across the river. In two hundred years the town—which by that time will be called Furnass—will number close to twenty thousand and will be thriving with the boom years of the American steel industry. There will be mills and factories up and down the river along which the town is built, the Allehela, and the river it flows into right below the town, the Ohio; the air will be thick and the sun hazy with smoke and billowing steam and clouds rising up the color of rust, the air will smell of coke and oil and sulfur; the hills on this side of the river will be stepped with narrow *frame houses with tall peaked roofs shouldered in among each other along narrow brick-paved streets, and there will always be the sound of machinery from the mills, of trains and towboats on the river and heavy trucks, of steel ringing on steel. In just twenty years after that, however, the boom years will be over, the mills will be closing or already shut down, and the people will be leaving again, those who can. Grass and new trees will be working their way up through cracks in the concrete, vacant lots will return to foxglove and Queen Anne's lace and trillium, a raccoon will think a deserted house high up on a dead-end street is its own. But all that's another story, a lot of different stories. . . .*

Today, here in the first days of autumn in the year 1764, there are only the two Highland soldiers struggling up the hillside. Behind them they can hear the army still at work crossing the ford in the river. The splash and cries of the animals, the shouts of the drovers, the shouts of the officers, the stroke, drag, and roll of the drums as the companies assemble on the bank and march off. They can hear it but they can't see it because of the thickets around them. Just as the army below can't see them. Around them there is only the sound of their own crashing through the brush, the buzz of insects, the cawing of a crow. Their own labored breathing. In front of them, of what they can see, there are only more thickets, and farther up the valley's hills, there are only more trees. A seemingly endless forest of white oak and maple and hickory. For an instant in their climb they reach for the same exposed tree root. The two men stop and look at each other, then take a deep breath and climb on. Neither one using that particular handhold after all. Deeper into the woods that will someday be Western Pennsylvania. Deeper into the wilderness that is called America. . . .

FLOWERS OF THE FOREST

1952

One

Charging up out of a ravine and across an open field, headed
right for him, was a troop of 2nd Dragoons, the Royal Scots
Greys—except that their horses were never gray, they were always white; he never understood that—sabers raised overhead
glinting in a patch of sunlight, guidons whipping in the wind,
horses stretched out at full gallop, the animals wild-eyed, frantic,
tails and manes flying, though the demeanor of the men in their
tall bearskins, considering the fact that they were riding into the
face of death, was curiously blank, expressionless, their eyes no
more than little black dots. Behind them, pouring through a
breach in the stone wall made by the enemy's cannonade or torn
down by their own sappers, came a detachment of the King's
Own Borderers, in tartan trews and white pith helmets, bayonets
fixed, running at full tilt, all of them in stride, all of them balanced incongruously on one leg with the other leg kicked out behind, as if each man were skating on a patch of green ice instead
of racing into battle; at the rear was a troop of Hussars, somber
in their brown uniforms with gold braid painted down the front
and their plumed shakos, their jackets worn like short capes over
their right shoulders, swords drawn but carried as if they were on

parade, their horses only at a trot, looking out of place and pointless, silly even, if this was supposed to be anything like a war, if
this was supposed to look at all real. The boy shifted his position,
moved around to the side of the display case hoping for a better
view, to get out of the glare of the doorway and away from his
own reflection in the glass, hoping to find a viewpoint where it
all seemed real again, where it was exciting and fun and he could
believe in it again.

The man's face appeared on the other side of the diorama,
grinning at him through the glass of the display case, as distract-
ing as his own reflection—more so because there was nothing he
could do to avoid it—hovering over the battle scene like some
oversized and sad-eyed moon, completely destroying the illusion.
The boy straightened up again and rested his elbows on top of
the counter.

The man stood behind the counter in the darkness of the store,
watching him, smiling. Bryce felt uncomfortable, the way the
man looked at him. He moved down the counter to look at
the other displays; he slid along sideways, leaning his elbows on
the glass top, his legs trailing along behind, feet crossing and
crisscrossing each other, his body slanted at an angle, so much so
that if the counter were suddenly removed he would have fallen
flat. The other cases contained military paraphernalia, cap
badges from various British regiments—Seaforth Highlanders,
Queen's Bays, the Buffs—as well as insignias and medals from
other countries, a Purple Heart and a Combat Infantryman
Badge from the United States, a Canadian Distinguished Service
medal, a red armband with a swastika and a lapel pin with the
twin lightning bolts of the SS.

"Now you're looking at the real stuff," Bob Bodner said from
behind the counter. "Say, I'll bet I've got something you'd like to
see."

He came around the end of the counter. The quickness of the man's movements startled him; Bryce lost his balance and almost toppled over. Bob Bodner put his hand on Bryce's shoulder as he passed—"You stay right there, son, stay right where you are"—as he squeezed behind Bryce in the narrow aisle, his hand lingering there perhaps longer than it needed to or should have, before he moved on toward the rear of the store.

It was a long narrow shoebox of a store, old and musty; two narrow aisles along its length, with shelves and tables—after the glass display counters at the front—stacked six- and eight-feet tall with boxes, kits for model planes, model cars and trucks, model ships, as well as jigsaw puzzles, board games—NOVELTIES, as it said on the front window—dolls, electric trains. Suspended over the aisles below the light fixtures, the milk-white globes that Bryce heard older kids say were shaped like breasts—Bryce wouldn't know, having never seen a breast; for that matter he wasn't even sure they were called breasts, having once overheard a conversation where he thought some boys talked about a woman's "tusks"—were strings of Halloween masks that hung there all year-round, the blank-eyed faces and gaping mouths of Frankenstein's monster and Count Dracula, monkeys and Uncle Sam. The wood floor was old and springy like a suspension bridge, as if the weight of walking on it would dump everything in the store in upon itself; the boards were splintery along the edges and warped into a series of ridges and valleys, a giant washboard, like the floor of the old Orchard Hill grade school before it was torn down.

Bob Bodner disappeared into the gloom at the rear of the store. A door opened somewhere, a light from a cellar stairway threw light and shadow swinging across the back wall of the store, a hulking shadow descended into the depths; from under the floor beneath Bryce's feet came the sounds of scraping and heavy objects being moved about. Bryce wondered if he should stick around, maybe the man forgot what he was going to do, maybe he went off to do something else. Some of the kids said Bob Bodner was an old fairy, though Bryce wasn't sure what that meant. The only thing he could piece together in his twelve-year-old mind was that being a fairy meant that Bob Bodner was rather small and flitted around a lot like Tinker Bell, but that didn't make much sense. Whatever, he knew it meant Bob Bodner wasn't very nice—maybe he should get out while he had the chance. He was a husky, lumpish boy, with limp brown hair that never went where it was supposed to, sticking up here, flopping down there; his face was still thick with baby fat and covered with preteenage acne, not the glaring white-headed peaks that other kids had but deep continuous blotches as if Bryce's pimples were upside down, their explosive heads pointed inward, which would later leave his cheeks waffled for life. Before he could make up his mind to leave however, Bob Bodner's shadow grew again on the back wall and then the light switched off and the door closed and the man came back out of the gloom again, his shoulders canted to fit down the narrow aisle, two-stepping along, dragging one foot though he wasn't lame, carrying a sword.

"This here's a genuine broadsword, the kind Colonel Bouquet's Highlanders carried when they came through this area in 1764, chasing the Indians into Ohio. Just feel that baby."

The sword was heavier than Bryce expected; he almost dropped it and speared his toe. The basket hilt encased his hand like a cage, delicate as wire lace; the red velvet inside the hilt was falling apart in shreds and smelly. Three grooves ran the length of the blade. Bryce held the weapon upright—it was nearly as tall as he was—jogged it up and down a couple times to get the feel of it, the weight.

"See how perfectly it's balanced?" Bob Bodner said as he took it back again. "It's meant for quick slashing strokes delivered by a stocky man. Those Highlanders were big fellows for their day but not by our standards, at best they were only five-seven or eight. Most men back then were five feet tall. Short little guys. And did you notice something else? The blade's not sharp, is it?"

Bryce pumped his shoulders once; he didn't know what Bob Bodner wanted him to say.

Bob Bodner smiled like a man vindicated. "I'll bet you thought it's because nobody sharpened it for a while, didn't you? Fact is the Highlanders didn't want their swords sharp. A broadsword's meant for downward, hacking strokes, down across the other guy's shoulder to open up the chest cavity. A sharp blade would get stuck in the bones."

To demonstrate, Bob Bodner took a step backward to give himself room, raised the sword and swung it at him, hacked the empty air a couple times above Bryce's shoulder. Bryce didn't think the man was actually going to hurt him, but something in Bob Bodner's expression—something savage, almost joyful in his eyes—scared him for a second. Bob Bodner relaxed a little, laughed as if he'd caught himself at something, as if a bad moment had passed; he rested the heavy blade on Bryce's shoulders, first one, then the other, as though saluting his valor, knighting him. For a brief second he touched the cool steel of the blade against Bryce's cheek. Then he carried the sword, point downward, back around the end of the counter, back into his cubbyhole behind the glass display cases where he normally waited for customers and collected their money.

"I like to see young people like yourself taking an interest in these military items," Bob Bodner said, not looking at him, busying himself putting the sword away in a corner beside his old rolltop desk. "You can't start too early to appreciate the significance of these things. This is history itself, right here in your hand. These are things that have gone into making the world what it is today. They make up a man's world. If I know somebody's serious about it, I can show him a whole lot of interesting stuff."

"You mean like these badges?" Bryce pointed down under the glass.

Bob Bodner waved the back of his hand through the air as if he were brushing away a cloud of gnats. "These are just the cheap things I keep up here on display. I've got the really valuable things down in the cellar. I've got racks and racks of it down there, swords, old flintlocks, I've even got complete uniforms down there."

"No kidding?"

"No kidding. I'll show them to you sometime if you're interested. But I can't during business hours, there's nobody else to look after the store. You come back some evening about closing time, five thirty, and I'll take you down there. There's a lot of things down there I could show a nice young boy like you."

"Gee, thanks." Bryce thought that response sounded like the kind of kid thing he was expected to say. He was thinking fast: he thought of spending his money on one of the badges to impress the man; he could tell that Bob Bodner was offering him something special from the intonation of his voice, something he didn't offer to just anybody, even though Bryce wasn't all that interested. But a junky old badge wasn't what he'd come for, what he had his heart set on. He pointed to one of the boxes of toy soldiers open on the shelf behind the counter. "I guess I'll take that set of the Black Watch."

It was the set he'd been waiting to buy, the set he wanted most of all, he had saved his money from cutting lawns for weeks to get it. He had waited to buy it until after he got the other sets he wanted, almost as if he were tempting fate—if it hadn't been here today, if it had been sold already, he would have cried— almost as if he were afraid of wanting it too much. Bob Bodner reached behind him and took the box from the shelf and put it on the glass countertop in front of Bryce. It was a long narrow shallow box, the metal figures inside strapped to the bottom with black elastic. There were four men with rifles resting on their shoulders, an officer with a drawn sword, and a piper, all on parade, their sporrans swinging in unison across the front of their painted kilts as they marched along, each one in a tall black bearskin with a red hackle. Bryce was relieved that the man didn't seem disappointed that he still wanted the toy soldiers.

"The Ladies from Hell," Bob Bodner said and closed the box and wrapped it in plain brown paper. "That's what they called the Black Watch during the First World War because they were so fierce. Did you know a Scotsman doesn't wear anything under his kilt? Nope, he's bare under there, what do you think of that? Must feel like a cold hand up under there every time the wind blows, huh? Ha ha."

He made a gesture like a hand reaching up under a kilt and feeling around, wriggling his fingers; when Bryce didn't say anything, Bob Bodner grew serious again. After Bryce paid his money, Bob Bodner handed him the package and then came around the end of the counter again and put his hand on Bryce's shoulder again.

"You know, I've got a piece of a real Black Watch kilt downstairs, I'll bet you'd really like to see that. We dug it up when we were excavating around the site of the old blockhouse down by the river. They must've buried one of their men here, you can still see the blood on it. . . ."

Just then the bell over the front door jangled and a small boy burst through the door and ran past them, plunging his hands into a jar of gum balls on one of the tables. He was followed by a woman in a housedress and floppy slippers who yelled, "Johnny, get out of there, get back here this instant or you won't get nothing at all." Bob Bodner dropped his hand from Bryce's shoulder and retreated back behind the counter as the woman slip-slopped by.

"I can't tonight," Bryce said, "I've got to get home. But maybe some other night. . . ."

Bob Bodner acted like he wasn't interested now, like he wasn't even sure what Bryce was talking about; the man shrugged and turned away and started leafing through some old invoices on his rolltop desk. Bryce stuck the box of soldiers under his arm and left.

Two

He giggled to himself as he ran and skipped along the sidewalk, heading up the main street toward home. Then he slowed down— running looked like he was afraid of something, and skipping was only for little kids, and girls. He was thrilled at the long-awaited treasure under his arm—it was his, it was finally his; from this day forward everything in his life would be right forever, everything in his life from this moment on would glow—and laughing to himself about Bob Bodner. Maybe he would go back some evening just to see if the man tried to do something to him; he was curious, he was sure whatever the man tried to do couldn't be that bad. Older people, parents and teachers, often said things about other people to scare kids to make them behave—in fact, Bryce hoped Bob Bodner tried to do something to him. He supposed the man would try to paw him a little, he had heard there were men like that; but that wouldn't be so awful. Bad things happened in the world, of course, but that was in worlds other than Bryce's and involved other kinds of people, bad people; Bob Bodner was nice to him, he was part of Bryce's world, it was inconceivable that the man would do anything to really hurt him. And it would make a great story. He could already see himself acting it out and making the other kids laugh. Bryce shuffled on, keeping an eye on the big house on the ridge of Orchard Hill, the

Sutcliff House, sitting among the trees on the bluffs a half mile
or so ahead of him overlooking the town, a landmark to home.

It was a warm afternoon in early summer though it had been
cloudy most of the day; sorties of black-gray clouds swept over
the hills and across the valley, with lighter puffs of gray like
bursts of flak trailing underneath, but that's all there was to it,
the clouds were only a threat, the rain never came. The town was
built along an S-curve in the river, bellied out within one arc of
the curve and squeezed in by the other as the town edged up the
slope on one side of the valley's hills. The town also stepped up
in three distinct levels as it paralleled the river—the Lower End;
the business district that everyone referred to as "downtown";
and Orchard Hill—and each successive level was looked on as a
better place to live, both by those who looked up as well as those
who looked down. Until recently, Bryce had spent most of his life
on Orchard Hill.

He had been aware as he was growing up of the steel mills in
town. The mills were a fact of life in Furnass, any part of Furnass,
the same as the hills and the river and the trees; there was
always the rust-covered smoke drifting over the valley, the steam
from the coke ovens billowing up like huge genies to dull the sun,
the massive buildings themselves blocking out or at least sharing
any view of the river from the town. At night the sky above the
town turned orange and red and yellow with flare-ups from the
Bessemer converters, and constellations of lights pinpointed the
towers and stacks. For that matter he was connected to the mills,
as was nearly everyone in town, because his father worked there,
though not in the mill itself. His father worked in the office, he
wore a white shirt and a suit to work, and office people at the
mill didn't belong to a union; it could have been an office anywhere, his father seemed as removed from what went on in the
mills, the dirt and the noise and the fire shooting up, as their
house on Orchard Hill seemed removed from the rest of the town.

But being this close to the mills, as close as he was now when he was downtown, was new to him. He had been downtown before, but always with his mother or father, when they were shopping or driving through on their way to someplace else, and he had never paid that much attention to the mills; it was only recently that he was allowed to come downtown on his own.

Here the steel mills—or mill to be exact, there was only one in the town, the Allehela Works of Buchanan Steel, that actually made steel, though there were a number of rolling and finishing and fabricating shops around it—were only a few blocks away from the main street, down at the bottom of the hill along the river. He knew he should be getting home, he wanted to get home too, he was anxious to open his package and look at his new soldiers, but he dawdled at the corner of each block, at the top of the steep brick-paved side streets leading down the hill, fascinated with the views of the mills and factories as he would have been with an intricate and highly detailed model train layout under a Christmas tree. Only a few blocks away workmen were moving around inside the gates, a tower crane unloaded coal and iron ore from barges along the river, a donkey engine pulled slag pots brimming with molten metal along the railroad tracks. The mouths of the Bessemers gaped like giant mortars aimed at the hills, at the town, at him. He could smell the sulfur and oil and smoke, the coke smoldering in the ovens; he could hear the rumble of the machinery, feel it all around him, the pounding of steel on steel. People on Orchard Hill, even his mother and father, said what terrible dreadful places the mills were, but he didn't understand what they meant. To him the mills seemed exciting and magical, something magnificent and grand. He hurried along from block to block, wondering what he'd see at the next corner.

It was close to four o'clock and the shifts were changing. The streets were clogged with cars, and mill hands climbed up the side streets, occasionally in clusters of twos and threes but more often than not by themselves, dragging themselves up against the pull of the steep sidewalks, too tired to talk, lunch pails and thermoses tucked under their arms, their eyes glazed, faces smeared or etched with soot, while other men, talking easily among themselves, kidding around, also with lunch pails and thermoses tucked under their arms, bouncing flatfooted against the pull of the same steep sidewalks, headed down the hill toward the main gate, ready for their turn. Along the main street the doors of the bars and taverns and social clubs stood open; inside the gloom lit by beer signs and jukeboxes, men lined the bars drinking their shot-and-a-beer—usually an "Imp-'n-Iron," the local favorite, Imperial whiskey and Iron City beer—some of the men drinking before their shift to make it through the time in the mill, others drinking after their shift to make it through the time at home. The bartenders had it timed: they poured out eight or ten shot glasses as the workmen began to straggle in and would fan those out across the bar; as the workmen downed the shots the bartenders pulled a like number of beers out of the cooler and would fan those out too in whichever directions the shot glasses had disappeared; then as the beer bottles in turn disappeared from the counter it would be time to refill the empty shot glasses that came sliding back at them again. Bryce had witnessed the ritual once when his father was on vacation and took his son with him while he stopped to have what he called a couple of horns. It was the first time Bryce had been aware that his life might be different from others in town. Even though the men all knew his father and said hello, Bryce was painfully aware that none of them talked to him for long or included him in their conversations— because these were mill hands, mill hunks, and his father was an office worker from Orchard Hill. Now Bryce kept an eye on the cars coming up the hill, just in case his father got out early today and he could catch a ride home, but he knew the office workers didn't usually get out until later. Toward the upper end of the main street, when traffic thinned out and he gave up the idea of seeing his dad and the views of the mill had lost their newness and fascination, Bryce crossed the street and climbed on up the hill into the back streets farther up the slope.

There was no reason to think that anyone was after him. The kids from Orchard Hill didn't get along with the kids from downtown, and vice versa—and neither group got along with the kids from the Lower End. In particular, the Orchard Hill kids didn't get along with the kids who lived at the foot of Orchard Hill, an area referred to as Locust Street, named for the street that ran along the base of the bluffs (the street in turn named for the tree, not for the bug). The kids from all three sections of town belonged to groups that called themselves or one another gangs, but they weren't street gangs as such with colors or turfs; they were only groups of kids who had grown up together and continued to hang around together and who stayed in their own sections of town most of the time; they had never organized into warring factions. But that didn't stop Bryce's imagination. This was hostile territory, enemy territory, and he was Jeb Stuart leading a cavalry raid deep into Northern territory—there were stories that the Confederate cavalry actually had raided the town—he was one of Bouquet's Highlanders scouting for signs of Indians in the woods. Just in case somebody gave him trouble, he figured he'd have less chance of running into any of the Locust Street kids if he kept away from the main thoroughfare and followed a zigzag course through the back streets and alleys, heading in the general direction of the wooden stairs that climbed the face of the bluff. The round corner tower of the Sutcliff House rose above the trees at the top of the bluff like a lighthouse, like a castle keep, guiding him to safety. He was half a block from the foot of the stairway, walking down the last alleyway, when somebody called to him.

"Hey Brycey-Brycey, where're you going in such a hurry?"

The boy's name was Chet; Bryce had seen him around at Little League and Stokers' football games but they had never said anything to each other, Bryce wasn't even sure of his last name. He was Bryce's age, maybe a year or two older, with a pointy squeezed-together face, the kind that seemed meant for poking into things. Chet came out from between two old wooden garages, holding a strip of licorice with both hands as he nibbled off the sugar buttons with his front teeth. He fell into step beside Bryce, matching him stride for stride, length for length. Bryce couldn't tell if the other boy was trying to make fun of him or trying to be funny.

"What're you doing way down here, Dicey-Brycey? I thought you Orchard Hill guys were scared you'd get your feet dirty if you came downtown."

"I had to run an errand. For my dad."

"That what's in the package?"

"Yeah. It's a tie."

"Let me see."

"I can't, it's all wrapped up. My mum's getting it for him. It's a present." Bryce held the box up in front of his shirt like a tie, clowning, wagging the end of the box back and forth pendulum-style and fluttering his eyebrows as if he were the height of fashion. "La-deda-deda."

"You're weird, Licey-Brycey."

"If I'm weird, you're even weirder, because you're the one talking to a weird person."

"Oh brother," Chet said and rolled his eyes.

Bryce thought he had the upper hand with the other boy. Chet gave up matching Bryce's strides and scuffled along in the dirt of the alley at his own pace, still teething the sugar buttons off the licorice strip, raising little clouds of dust and gravel with his floppy tennis shoes. Bryce sidled over beside Chet and began to mimic *his* walk; he shuffled his feet even harder and raised even larger clouds of dust and gravel—the gravel sprayed out in front of them, pinging off garbage cans and a car parked in front of a garage door—humming a senseless tune through his nose like Mortimer Snerd, "Tum de-tum de-tum," in time with their steps. Chet danced away from him backward, tripping over his own feet and almost falling, as if Bryce had physically assaulted him.

"Boy, you are weird!"

Bryce slopped on, humming louder and acting dumber than ever, feeling like he had won something.

Scattered along the alley were dozens of green crab apples—some rotting, some squashed by passing cars, some pecked by birds, some freshly fallen and whole—from trees in the backyards; one yard was nearly covered with the wild apples, impossible to walk across, the area permeated by the thick tart smell. He had heard his friend Julian's father say that there were wild apple trees all through this area at one time, the same way that there were once locust trees, before the town spread this far from the river; the first people who built here cut down the locusts but left as many of the crab apples as they could, considering themselves lucky to have the apples for pies and preserves; Julian's father said the people who lived here now thought the people who built here then were crazy. Chet, a few yards ahead of him, kicked at the apples in his path, thudding them into garage doors and fences. When a cat stuck its head out from some bushes, the boy picked up an apple and winged it at the animal, just missing it.

"Hey, don't do that," Bryce said.

Chet's eyes lit up. "What's the matter, Icey-Brycey, afraid I'll hurt it? Awww, the poow wittle ting. . . ."

He laughed and picked up another rotting apple and threw it in the direction where the cat disappeared, then fired off another at a robin in a tree before the bird flew away. Bryce kept on walking, back to his normal pace again, trying to ignore the other boy, wanting to distance himself from him; he didn't know what else to do, he wanted to run at Chet and hurl himself at him, flail at him, beat him up, but suppose he did run at him and Chet didn't move, wasn't afraid of him, then what would he do? He was almost to the end of the alley, the wooden steps up the hillside were right ahead across Locust Street. But Chet came shuffling after him, sliding his feet to kick up more clouds of dust, flopping the licorice belt around in one hand as if he carried a dead snake while holding a crab apple in the other.

"Hey, you ever try to eat one of these?"

"You can't eat a crab apple," Bryce said, walking backward a few steps before turning around again, "everybody knows that. They're poison or something. Like buckeyes."

"I can eat buckeyes too." Chet stopped and looked at the crab apple in his hand for a second, rubbed it against his shirt, then took a bite out of it. He chewed it a couple times before the sour taste got too much for him and he had to spit it out.

"Told ya," Bryce called over his shoulder and headed across the brick-paved street toward the steps. The Sutcliff House had disappeared behind the trees at the top of the bluff now, he couldn't see it this near to the hillside, but knowing it was close by made him feel safe already, under the protection of the guns from a castle wall, he was almost back on Orchard Hill again, home. He wanted to run but held himself back.

"Hey, what's that?" Chet said. "What's going on?"

Bryce wondered too. The long wooden stairway in front of him was empty—there were a hundred steps, interspersed with five landings on which to stop and catch your breath, climbing straight up the hillside, the wood railings canted toward each other as they neared the top like a model of perspective and parallel lines—but off to the left there was movement among the trees and bushes, figures moving along the crisscross trails that webbed the face of the bluff, eight or ten boys making their way Indian file across the steep hillside, toward the woods and the steeper sandstone cliffs on the back side of the hill away from town. He relaxed again when he recognized Sonny Rourke and the Binder brothers and some of the older kids from the Hill—it wasn't part of the Locust Street gang, they weren't going to chase him if they saw him. He started up the steps but Chet ran after him and grabbed his arm.

"Come on, don't you want to see what they're up to?"

"Nah, they probably don't want anybody else hanging around." The other boys disappeared into the brush and trees. It would never occur to Bryce to try to follow them; when the older kids went off somewhere like that it usually meant they were getting into some kind of trouble. "Besides, I got to get home."

"Chickenshit, chickenshit," Chet punched him on the arm and ran past him up the steps to the first landing and crawled through the railing after the others.

Bryce dragged up the steps, watching him go; as he climbed he tapped the toe of one shoe behind the other on each tread to hear it clunk against the old wood, thinking about how much he wanted to be home and go up to his room alone and look at his new soldiers. But when he got to the first landing he climbed through the railing too and followed the trail where the other boys had gone.

Three

When he caught up to the others, they were standing in a cluster on the hillside, behind the billboard for Town Talk Bread, on a ridge overlooking Walnut Bottom Road that ran along the base of the valley's hills. The leader seemed to be Brownie—the older boys called him Needle-Prick Brown the Insect Fucker; Bryce wasn't sure what that meant but he was pretty sure it wasn't a nice thing to say—who was trying to get the others to line up.

"Come on, you guys, a little order here, a little order. Got to have a line, got to have a line, there's plenty for everybody if we can just get this organized, this isn't no picnic where we might run out of potato salad or something. Unless of course you were planning on doing some eating too but that's something I'd strongly discourage, strongly discourage, unless you're the first one in line and even then I'd personally take a dim view of such proceedings, yes sir, a very dim view. You never know where that hamburger's been today already—hey Brycey, what're you doing here, aren't you a little young for this kind of thing?"

Bryce blushed as the other boys turned to look at him. He couldn't say anything, he shifted his package from one hand to the other.

"Let him stick around," Harry Todd said. "How do you know, maybe Bryce is the biggest stud on Orchard Hill." He laughed, directing his laugh around at the others as if it were a signal for them to laugh too. They laughed too.

Bryce's understanding of "stud" was as imperfect as it was of anything else having to do with the subject of sex; he figured Harry Todd meant that all the Orchard Hill kids stood together like the wooden uprights inside a wall—his father had looked for a stud once, tapping around the walls of the living room all one Saturday afternoon looking for a place to hang a picture—and the joke was to call Bryce the biggest stud when he was actually smaller than anyone else there. Bryce thought it was a pretty good joke.

"Yeah, yeah, maybe so, maybe so," Brownie said, clapping his hands a couple times to get their attention again. "Okay, the little guys can stay but they'll have to be at the end of the line, can't take any chances, don't want to give the wrong impression about Orchard Hill guys, right? ha ha, just in case Bryce isn't the world's biggest stud. Okay then, come on, line up here, get your dollars ready and your pants off. I'll be the ticket taker, the conductor on this bus, ring-ring, fares please, no transfers, the

Brownie Express will take you to paradise, let the first passenger step forward and take a ride. . . ."

Brownie was older than the other kids on Orchard Hill; he was undoubtedly too old to be called a kid at all, though nobody was too sure just how old he was. He had dropped out of high school some years before to join the Marines and, according to his stories at least, had traveled all over the world. He was back in high school now, but his main interest seemed to be in teaching his young buddies all the stuff he'd learned while he was away. In a part of town where most kids' fathers were office workers or professional people or taught at the local college, Brownie's father drove a bus for Onagona County Transit; his family lived on the back side of the hill, along Walnut Bottom, in a house that was more like a cabin beside the creek with several rusting cars sitting in the yard. Brownie was thin and wiry, with a cue-ball haircut that helped create the impression that his head was too small for his body. Bryce usually stayed away from him, at the pickup baseball games at the Orchard Hill field or when they played touch football in the street in front of Sonny Rourke's house, or in the evenings when all the kids, young and old, gathered on the steps in front of Cane's Candy Store to watch the cars going up and down Orchard Avenue. Brownie acted crazy, no one knew what he was going to do next, which was why the other kids said they liked Brownie; what bothered Bryce most about Brownie was the look in his eyes, the way he looked at people, as if he might bite or kiss somebody at any moment. Standing off to one side of the line of boys, Bryce watched to see what they were going to do. It was then he noticed a guy he didn't recognize sitting on the ground in front of the others. Then he realized that the guy was a girl, and that she didn't have any pants on.

"Jeez, that's Chucky Bossick's sister!" Chet said.

"Chester, don't you go saying anything about this to Chucky," the girl said when she looked up and saw Chet.

"Hey, how'd that Locust Street kid get here?" Dave Binder said.

Herman the German tried to grab Chet but the younger boy dodged away and ran back along the trail toward the steps.

"Shit," the girl said, "now he'll tell my brothers for sure."

"You just worry about the humping," Brownie snapped. "There's enough of us here to take care of both you and your brothers."

Bryce was confused and must have looked it. Harry Todd drifted over and sat on the ground near him; as he took off his pants along with the others, he looked up at Bryce and grinned.

"Old Brownie's something, isn't he? He talked Carla Bossick into taking all of us on, and he even gets a split of the money. Brownie certainly has a way with the women."

Bryce grinned back as if that explained everything all right, but he was more bewildered than ever. Davy Binder was the first one with his pants off. He paid Brownie a dollar and then went over and lay on top of Carla between her legs and humped up and down a few times while the other guys all yelled encouragement. Then he got off and Brucie Willoughby paid his dollar and went over and took his turn while Davy Binder got another dollar out of his pants and went to stand at the back of the line. Brownie stood near Carla, giving a running commentary.

"Yes sir, yes sirree, I always say that every young man should participate in at least one gang bang during his lifetime. Of course to be a true gang bang you should actually have to hold the girl down and nobody's ever had to hold Carla down yet, and besides I happen to know she wants the money to buy a new dress or something—"

"You son-of-a-bitch, Brownie," Carla raised her head over Brucie Willoughby's shoulder. "You promised not to say anything about that—"

"—so we'll just have to pretend the girl isn't quite such a willing participant. Yes sir, take it from ol' Needle-Prick Brown the Insect Fucker himself, this is a rite of passage, an introduction into those classic virtues of war, rapine, and plunder, we're in touch with history here, guys. You know, I think I'm going to design a coat of arms for myself, a big horny foot resting on an endless field of tits. . . ."

From where Bryce stood, he couldn't see what was going on very well; he only got a good look at the other boys as they rolled off Carla and went to take the last place in line again, their dinks sticking up or sticking out, bigger than he ever knew dinks could be. At first he wondered if there was something wrong with his dink, his certainly never looked like that—how was he to know? He'd never seen anybody else's dink that he could remember; that his was different would explain so many other things too, why he always felt different from the other kids, why he never seemed to fit in—then he pieced together the theory that their dinks got that large as a result of what they did on top of Carla. He reasoned that she held their dinks somehow between her legs while the guys humped up and down and that stretched their dinks until they got big—sort of like pulling taffy. When he moved a little closer he still couldn't see her dink when the guys got off her; he guessed she pulled her dink back out of the way between her legs. Then he saw that each guy's dink was that big before they lay down on top of her—how did they do that? He sat down on the hillside, his package of toy soldiers upside down on the grass beside him, mystified and sad. He would never understand how things worked in the world; he knew his dink would never be able to do anything like that. Despite all the hooting and hollering going on around him, he felt very lonely.

After a while he got tired of watching, tired of trying to figure it all out. Beyond the billboard, the hillside curved around toward the hills on this side of the valley, the wooded slope in places dropping off over steep sandstone cliffs; below, a car moved along Walnut Bottom Road, while at the foot of the bluffs, among some factory buildings, a forklift loaded pallets of boxes into a freight car, a workman wrestled a fifty-gallon drum onto a rack, a crew drove spikes along the rails of a spur though this far away there was no sound to accompany the swing of the hammers. Above the hills, the gray clouds piled up in the sky like a twenty-car collision. Nobody else in the world was in the least concerned about what was going on behind the billboard, nobody else considered it earth-shattering or in the least important, why should he care? Bryce sat there, pulling up clumps of grass from between his legs and flipping them over the hillside; he was only vaguely aware that the other boys were through, comparing performances as they put their pants on again. It took him a moment to realize that Carla was talking to him.

"Hey, what's the matter with you, can't you hear?"

"What?"

"I said, 'Hey, don't you want to do it too?'"

Carla was sitting up with her bare legs spread—she was really good at hiding her dink—her open crotch aimed his direction. Her voice was gravelly and tough, but she seemed friendly. Bryce shook his head.

"I'd let you, if you wanted to. You might as well." She pulled up a clump of grass herself from between her legs and flipped it away. "You're cute. I'll bet you never had a girl before, did you? I'll bet you're not even old enough."

"I don't know," Bryce said.

"Hey Carla, leave the kid alone," Herman the German said. "Ain't you had enough already?"

"Go screw yourself. I was talking to the kid."

"I don't have to go screw myself, I just screwed you."

"Nyah-nyah-nyah," Carla said and gave him the finger. She turned back to Bryce. "Don't pay any attention to them, they're a bunch of jerks."

"Then why'd you let them do . . . that?"

"There's nothing wrong or dirty about it, if that's what you mean. People only say that because they're jealous or they don't get enough of it themselves and don't want anybody else to get any either, you know? Or maybe they're scared or something. I think it's kind of fun. It's okay."

Bryce was in love with her. He always thought of girls in terms of who he wanted to marry; he always imagined himself married to them already and living together in a big house and dancing a lot while an orchestra played the way couples did in Fred Astaire movies. Carla had dark dry scraggly hair that hung halfway down her back and the kind of button nose and knobby cheeks his mother called a Hunky face, but Bryce didn't care. He wanted to take her away from here; he didn't know exactly what was going on but he knew it wasn't nice. He wanted to chase away all the other kids and put his coat around her—he wasn't wearing a coat but that's what the hero always did in the movies when he found a girl without her clothes—and take her away someplace where they would always be happy.

But all he could think to say was, "Doesn't it hurt you, when they do that?"

"You hear that, you jerks?" she called out. "He's the only one in the whole bunch of you who cares whether it hurts me or not."

"That's because he's only a kid," Sonny Rourke said.

"It doesn't hurt you and you know it," one of the other guys said. "You love it."

"You just think I love it," Carla said and looked out over the hollow. "It takes a little kid like this to show you guys how to be considerate of a girl."

"We'd be considerate if you were worth it."

"Come on, Brycey, get out of here," Brownie said, getting up from the others and coming over. "You're bad for business, you're making the merchandise start to think too much. She's liable to sprain something and hurt herself."

Brownie reached down, either to help him up or drag him to his feet, when something whizzed through the trees above their heads. Everyone stopped and looked around, looked at each other. Then there was another and another, this time closer. The next one was followed by Bob Binder howling with pain. Some of the boys jumped to their feet, some ducked close to the ground.

"Watch out!"

"There! Over there!"

"They're throwing things at us!"

"Jesus, it's my brothers!" Carla screamed and reached for her clothes.

Four

Coming across the face of the slope, through the bushes and trees, were a dozen boys or more from Locust Street, carrying crab apples—some by the armful and some in bags and some in bushel baskets that two boys lugged between them—running forward and then stopping to hurl some of their ammunition at Brownie and the others and then running forward again. One of the apples crashed through the branches of a tree overhead, sprinkling Bryce with leaves and twigs. Another hit Sonny Rourke in the face, the half-rotten fruit splattering on impact and opening a cut over his eye; the boy screamed with pain and collapsed in the bushes. Carla tried to escape, pulling on her jeans as she ran, down the side of the hill toward the bluffs, but her brother Chucky, in his Furnass Stokers football jersey, ran past Bryce and grabbed the girl and cuffed her on the back of the head, sending her facedown in the dirt. He was about to kick her when Brownie, screaming at the top of his voice, wild-eyed, hurdled over a bush and tackled the other boy, landing on top of him and pounding him on the side of the head. Two Locust Street boys slid down the slope between the trees and jumped Brownie but Brownie threw them off and grabbed a dead tree limb on the ground and went after them swinging it like a baseball bat.

Bryce couldn't move, he was frozen to the spot, not afraid for himself but horrified and sickened by what was going on around him, at the transformation, the savagery and the violence that had come over the boys on both sides. Among the attackers Chet ran among the older boys, kicking at any of the Orchard Hill kids who were down, throwing crab apples and buckeyes at kids who weren't looking his direction. When he saw Bryce he picked up a stone and threw it at him, missing his head by inches, but Bryce still couldn't move. Then Chet turned and fled as Harry Todd came running over and grabbed Bryce by the arm and started to pull him up the hill.

"Wait, my package!" Bryce said and picked up the soldiers and then scrambled on up the hillside, Harry Todd right behind him, the older boy pushing him on through the brush and a patch of huckleberry and up the steep broken slope until they were away from the fighting.

They continued to scramble up some outcroppings of sandstone, Harry Todd leading the way now, reaching back to give Bryce a hand, and on through some more dense bushes until they came to one of the crisscross trails. They followed it across the face of the hillside and up through a hedgerow of trees of heaven and came out of the woods at the edge of the Sutcliffs' long backyard. Behind them, back down the bluff, there were faint sounds of the fight still going on, boys yelling at each other, crashing about. As the two of them started across the manicured lawn toward the house, Harry Todd laughed.

"That was something, wasn't it? I thought I better get you out of there. I was afraid somebody was going to cream you."

"Don't you think we should do something?"

Harry Todd looked at him. Everybody said Harry Todd was the best-looking guy in town; he had blond hair and blue eyes, like the pictures in the magazines of California surfers, and was the darling and dream of every girl in school. Bryce was sure the only reason Carla Bossick agreed to let all those other guys do that to her wasn't because Brownie talked her into it, but because she knew that Harry Todd was going to be one of the guys—it was the only way she could ever get somebody like Harry Todd Sutcliff. Harry Todd was only a couple of years ahead of Bryce in school—Harry Todd already went downtown to the junior high school—but he seemed much older to Bryce, not only one of the older kids but almost a grown-up, with a kind of glamor about him; though Harry Todd was around occasionally when Bryce came over to the house to play with Harry Todd's younger brother Dickie, Bryce had never talked to him alone like this, one to one, and it made him feel older and important. Harry Todd shrugged and tucked half the length of his fingers into the pockets of his jeans.

"What's there to do about it?"

"I don't know. Shouldn't we call the police or something?"

"Nah. Stuff like this goes on all the time, it's the same old story. Now somebody'll get some more of our guys and we'll all go back down to Locust Street and chase their guys around, and then they'll get some more of their guys and they'll come up here and chase us. That'll go on the rest of the afternoon until it gets dark and everybody goes home, and then tomorrow we'll sit around and talk about what a great fight it was and everybody will more or less forget about it until somebody like Brownie stirs it up again. You're just lucky you haven't got mixed up in one of these fights before."

"I guess. But won't some of those guys down there get hurt?"

They were at the steps to the back door. It was a large red-brick house, three stories tall, with a large porch extending across the front and around the side, dormer windows like lookouts on the slate roof, and the round corner tower—like a castle sitting on the edge of the hill, looking out over this end of the valley, everyone in town knew it—the grandest house on Orchard Hill, which meant the grandest house in Furnass. Harry Todd paused in midstride on the steps, one leg on the step above the other.

"Yeah, sure. Some of our guys'll probably get hurt, and some of their guys too, but that's the way it is. Me, I try to stay out of these things as much as possible—I don't want to mess up my good looks, you know? I mean, why disappoint all the girls, right? ha ha. But guys like Brownie love it. He'll probably be up here pretty soon with a gash on his head or something but that won't stop him. He'll get a couple Band-Aids and I'll help patch him up and then he'll be raring to go again. Guys like Brownie, they don't care what happens, to them or anybody else. I'll tell you something else, most guys you'll run into are like that too, they don't give a shit about anything. But you better get yourself home now. I think we're going to lose this one today, which means there'll be Locust Street kids running all over the place up here, and they won't care if you're a fighter or younger than they are or nothing."

"Okay, thanks. See ya." Bryce tucked his package under his arm and headed across the wide front yard and down the slope of the terrace. On the dead-end street his shoes tick-tacked in the fresh oil until he came to the pavement at the end of the block. He lived half a dozen blocks away, across Orchard Hill beyond Covenant College, on the edge of the bluffs that overlooked the railroad yard and the river and the steep wooded hillside on the other side of the valley. It was a small frame house—a narrow two-story, three-rooms-in-a-row house, with a tall peaked roof—covered with Insulbrick the color of dried blood or spilled grape juice. Except for how it might be painted or covered with siding, the house was identical to any number of small frame houses in Furnass; it was a company house, built for a laborer's family at the turn of the century when Orchard Hill was no place special and even a bit inconvenient because it was so far away from the mills. When Bryce was past the college and a few doors away from home, a couple of Locust Street kids on bicycles came around the corner at the end of the block. They hollered and charged toward him, pedaling furiously, then jumped off their bikes and started throwing crab apples from the shopping bags they carried on the handlebars. Bryce took off running across the neighbors' yards. As he made it to safety inside his front door, apples thudded against the porch and clanked a metal lawn chair. He peeked between the curtains on the door. Outside the boys got back on their bikes and circled around in the middle of the street a couple of times, waving their fists and hooting with triumph, before they sped away.

"Is that you, Bryce?" his mother called from the kitchen.

"Yes, Mum."

"Your father called to say he's going to be late."

"Okay, Mum."

Which meant his father had stopped to have his couple of horns on the way home; it was anyone's guess what time he'd get there. Bryce could eat whenever he wanted to, all he had to do was to tell his mother when, but he wasn't hungry. The downstairs of the house was dark on the gray day, as dark as if it were raining outside, the living room and hallway and dining room gloomy. The only light was the glow leaking out around the kitchen door. His mother would be sitting in the glare of the overhead light at the kitchen table, drinking one of her endless cups of coffee, smoking one cigarette after another, coughing into her hand, the smoke hanging in the air of the room as thick as the days when the smoke from the mills wouldn't rise and settled back over the town, listening to the radio—*Young Widder Brown, Mary Noble Backstage Wife*—and playing solitaire. He wanted to talk to her, tell her something about what happened today, what he saw, but he didn't know what he wanted to say; he didn't understand what happened to him today, though it certainly felt as though something had. But she never seemed that interested in the things he told her. The more he thought about it, the less he wanted to tell her anything that happened to him today or ever; there didn't seem to be anything she could say about it that would make the least bit of difference to him. He went upstairs to his room.

He sat on the bed and unwrapped the package, released the soldiers, the six marching Highlanders of the Black Watch, from the black elastic bands that held them in the box; he set them in place on the floor with the others of his collection. On his portable phonograph he picked out his favorite track on the record of bagpipe music, "Flowers of the Forest." Then as the drone and skirl of a lone piper keened through the room, Bryce lay on his stomach on the floor, his chin resting on his hands so he was at the soldiers' level, to see the scene he'd created, the results of what he'd worked and saved for, what he'd daydreamed about for months.

Sentries lined the towers of the castle, keeping watch along the walls and balustrades, their bayonets fixed. In the courtyard the band of the Coldstream Guards was lined up, ready for the review. Squads of foot soldiers, Grenadier and Irish Guards, in their red tunics and tall black bearskins, some presenting arms, some kneeling and ready to fire in case of an attack, were in formation on either side of the drawbridge, while mounted detachments of the 12th Royal Lancers and the Queen's Own Hussars scouted the plains beyond the castle walls. The colors flew from the highest tower; there was no wind, the banners and guidons were motionless on their standards. All eyes were turned down the great canyon, down the towering cliffs toward the river where a relief column of the Black Watch came into view, gaining the bank of the river, marching to the skirl of the pipes . . . but it was no good. It meant nothing to him now. The plain was the dusty hardwood floor; the wall of the canyon was his bed; the riverbank was the edge of the rug in the hallway; and he was lying on the floor of his bedroom, the cracks of the floorboards mounting away from him like the lines of an enormous tablet. He was almost thirteen years old. Almost a teenager. Next year he wouldn't be going to the nice safe grade school there on Orchard Hill; next year he'd be going to junior high, downtown with all the other kids in town, kids from Locust Street and the Lower End, even black kids. And here he was, playing with a bunch of little toy soldiers. He got up and turned off the phonograph and went back downstairs.

His hand trailed down the rungs of the banister like he was plucking the strings of a wooden harp, *tunk tunk tunk*. The down-stairs rooms were even darker now with the approach of evening though the windows still glowed a muted gray. From the kitchen—the outline of the door flared with light in the poorly fitted frame—came the sound of his mother's radio with the latest news. Outside there were voices, yelling. He parted the filmlike sheers on the window of the front door with the edge of his hand. Boys were running through the yards and along the street, chasing each other, throwing crab apples and buckeyes and stones at one another, boys from Locust Street and Orchard Hill, though he couldn't tell who was chasing whom, who was winning or losing.

He opened the door and walked out on the front porch. Most of them were already gone, around the corner at the end of the block, but two boys on bicycles—the two who had chased him earlier—were parked by the curb a few houses away, catching their breath and talking, their backs to him. Bryce went down

the walk and picked up a crab apple from the grass; he weighed
it in his hand for a moment, then snuck closer to the boys on the
bicycles, crouching across his yard and through the neighbor's
yard along the hedge. When he was close enough he stood up and
threw the crab apple, hitting one of the boys in the back. He
walked out from the hedge and stood in the sidewalk, waiting—
he sang a little song, at first to himself to buck himself up and
then out loud, sang it at the other boys like a challenge, making
it as dumb as he could, "Do-dedo-dedo-dedo . . ." and danced up
and down, clowning—to make sure they saw who threw it as they
wheeled their bikes around and came charging toward him. Then
he started to run, up the street to join the others.

. . . There is a gunshot from the river behind them. The two sol-
diers on the hillside stop, look at each other. Wait. But the distant
sounds of the drums and the herded animals and the pack train
continue down in the valley. It was probably one of the militiamen
firing off his rifle for the fun of it, despite Colonel Bouquet's strict
orders not to, despite the threat of five hundred lashes with the
cat-o'-nine-tails. It's not an attack. It's not Indians. The two
Highlanders struggle on up the slope.

They stop to catch their breath on a bluff overlooking the river,
stand panting for a few moments in the stark autumn sunlight.
Farther up the slope, looking up through the trees, the leaves are
a bright ceiling, all yellow and red and orange. Back down the
hillside, looking down through a break in the trees, over the top
of the forest, the leaves are a bright carpet extending over the
endless rolling hills. Along the bank of the river, stretched out
along the S-curve of the river through the valley, is the column of
Bouquet's army, marching away from them. The first units are
already out of sight, around the hills at the far end of the valley,
continuing their march along the Ohio River deeper into the wil-
derness. Into the stronghold of Pontiac's Indians in the Ohio ter-
ritories, where few white men have ever gone before and certainly
no army, to demand peace or to win it, once and for all. At the
crossing on the Allehela, the last soldiers are wading across the
ford. Their kilts petal out around them in the water, looking from
this height like a scattering of flowers. In the distance, the pipes
keen against the valley's hills.

The older man, a corporal of grenadiers, turns to resume the
climb. The younger, a private in the light infantry, holds up his
hand to tell the other to wait a minute. While the corporal
watches, the private leans his musket against a tree. Slips the
leather crossbelt off his shoulder, holds the end of his long plaid

*between his knees, and takes off the scarlet tunic. Leaving him in
a tattered and much-stained linen blouse. He adjusts his plaid and
the crossbelt on his shoulder again, and tucks the wadded-up tunic
under the crossbelt at the back. The whole time he watches the
corporal's face, his eyes. Not really challenging him but waiting
to be challenged, waiting to be ordered to put the tunic back on.
But the corporal doesn't say anything. Only when the private is
ready to go again does the corporal rap him on the arm, keeping
the silence between them. The corporal motions with his hand
that he, the corporal, will lead the way, and that he, the private,
will follow. That understood, they continue up the hillside, single
file, into the trees. Looking for lost sheep. . . .*

MAKING DO

1976

One

"I don't believe this," Jerry said, looking around his living room. "I finally get a day off, and this is what I get?"

It looked like the scene of a massacre: in the living room his wife was crumpled up in the recliner, his daughter was spread-eagled on the sofa, his granddaughter was curled into herself in the middle of the hooked rug on the floor. They were supposedly watching some game show on television, but none of them seemed to notice, or care, that the color was awful, that everything had a purplish cast, except for the faces that were decidedly green.

"For Christ's sake," he said from the archway, not wanting to go in any farther. He raised his can of Iron City at them. "It's my first day off in two weeks."

His wife leaned around the corner of the recliner (it was supposed to be *his* chair), one arm thrown over the side, fleshy side up, like a dead fish; as usual when she talked to him, she looked his general direction but her eyes crossed slightly and didn't focus.

"Jerry, why don't you go do something?"

"What do you want me to do?"

"I don't know. Do something. Anything. You're always complaining you never have time to do anything. Now you have the time."

"But I don't want to do just anything. It's my day off."

"You're the one who wants to work the overtime and extra days."

"So okay, today I'm not working the overtime and extra days. I want to do something special for my day off."

"Then do it. Find something. *Capisce?*" Reina shook her head—impossible man—pulled in her arm and disappeared back into the chair again. Back to the television.

The talk show host was interviewing some guy with an English accent. Great: he finally gets a day off and all his family wants to do is watch one guy who looks like a pansy talk to another guy with an English accent (and they were both green, for Christ's sake). He might as well have worked a double shift, made some extra money.

Oh well. He stretched, traced with the fingertips of his free hand the arc of the doorway up to the point over his head, scowled on general principle at the three females in the room (they didn't pay any attention), and turned away. He wandered, Iron City in hand, back through the downstairs of the house, visiting the dining room, kitchen, the back bedroom where he and Reina slept, like a visitor to some curio shop. The house was full of knickknacks—junk, as Jerry made a point to call it—Reina collected things the way some people stole. Salt and pepper shakers, little bells, thimbles, ceramic figures (dogs, ladies in fine dresses, drunks leaning on lampposts, cutesy little boys fishing), plates, teacups (with or without saucers), coffee mugs (with or without handles), what have you. She filled every shelf he built for her with the things she found at flea markets and secondhand shops and garage sales; sometimes he wondered why he kept building shelves for her. As if that wasn't enough, she covered every remaining space on the walls of the kitchen and hallway with letters, greeting cards, articles she clipped from the newspaper, snapshots. He never would admit it to Reina, but he was always curious to see her latest additions to the refrigerator. The only thing he thought was new was an *Andy Capp* cartoon—ha ha, very funny. Back in the archway to the living room again, he stopped long enough to shake his head at his brood and give them a good disgusted *tsk*, but they still didn't pay any attention to him. He carried his Iron City on down the narrow hallway beside the second-floor stairs and out to the front porch.

He sat on the top step, lifted up his T-shirt to feel the warm air on his skin, to smack his bare belly a couple of times. Lean and mean—*Smack! Smack!*—that was the way he liked to describe himself. At fifty, he still had all his hair, molded into the same pompadour he wore in high school; most of it was still the color of sand too. Just a little gray. He also liked to say that the reason he stayed so slim—his body was slight as if he were a trifle smaller than life-sized—was because he worked so hard. The guys he worked with at the mill, the guys who knew him, knew different—guys for the most part he grew up with in Furnass, or knew of growing up—always laughed at that, but it was okay, he said it to be funny; it was a point of pride with him that he didn't work as hard as the other guys on the crew, that he found ways around it. In general celebration of himself, he took another swallow of beer.

At the end of the street, half a block away, a cloud of steam billowed up from the mill, momentarily blocking the sun. Not his problem. Reina was right; there were a number of things he could do today. Should do today. He should trim up the coffin-sized patch of grass that passed for a yard, he hadn't done that in weeks. For another, the Insulbrick had pulled off the side of the house in a couple of spots; underneath, the wood was rotting from being covered in the first place, he needed to do something about that. Today would be a good day to replace the gutters too, fix the screens. The truck needed a tune-up. There were any number of things he could do. It wore him out just to think of them all.

It was a small narrow two-story frame house in the Lower End of Furnass, in one of the several patches of small frame houses in this part of town among the factories and warehouses, close by the buildings that were once the Keystone Steam Works and were now part of Buchanan Steel, in a part of town known as Lock because it was near the falls and the old lock on the river. In a vacant lot nearby stood one of the massive piers supporting the viaduct across the end of valley, the great arc of the bridge spanning away like a concrete rainbow. There were fewer houses in this part of town now than when he grew up here—in a house two doors down—and the yards around the remaining houses were larger because of the number that had been abandoned and leveled or simply collapsed. In his own yard, surrounded by a picket fence that he'd never got around to painting and that by this time consisted of mainly broken or missing pickets, were piles of lumber, roofing material, gutters and flashing; today would be a good time to finish the porch too, he should get right at it. Last summer he got as far as jacking up this end; the rest of the porch clung to the house the best it could. But today was his day off, for Christ's sake.

A man was walking up the center of the street, keeping to the rims of the potholes—which were sizable, some more like craters, the street looked bombed. Jerry was used to guys walking through, the mill employed close to twenty thousand people after all. And he was used to blacks in Lock and the Lower End, he had grown up playing in their houses and they'd played in his and he had never thought much about it. What was there to think about? That was the way things were, that's all, no use thinking otherwise, nothing to be gained. But this guy, in jeans and a work shirt like anybody else, looked Indian, an India Indian of all things. Jerry nodded, mouthed hello without making a sound, the custom of the country; the man nodded in return and kept walking. The guy must live somewhere in the neighborhood —what little neighborhood was left—but Jerry had no idea where; next thing he supposed there would be all kinds of foreigners moving in—Cambodians, for Christ's sake, Cubans, boat people, fifty-seven varieties of Chinkaderos and Gonorrheans. Just his luck, of course; they'd all say Hey, let's go live around ol' Jer, he doesn't have enough grief in his life. Not that he minded exactly; it was to be expected, one more fact of life. He started to take another pull of his Iron City when he found Stephie staring into the side of his head. How long had she been standing there?

"Well hello, pumpkin. How come you're no good?"

"I don't know." His granddaughter, age eight, hung her head, put one dirty bare foot on top of the other; her bikini showed mostly flesh-covered bones.

"Your head's too big and your stomach sticks out and your feet don't match." It was usually good for a giggle, but apparently not today.

"Can I have a sip of beer?"

"Beer's only for grown-ups."

She thought about that for a moment. "Can I have a sip?"

He handed her the can. She took five healthy guzzles before he grabbed it back again.

"Jeez, I didn't say you could have the whole thing."

The little girl wiped her lips on her bare arm.

"Stephie!" her mother bellowed, five feet away from them, standing behind the rusty screen door. Ro was in her early thirties, with short black hair and the remains of teenage acne and her mother's plump features gone blunt. "Dad, did you give her some of that?"

"Yes, I gave her some of that," he mocked her tone. He looked off down the street, away from the mill, toward the river and the falls and the remains of the old canal, though he couldn't see any of them from here. He had lived on the street for so long that he also never saw the lush green wall rising up on the other side of the valley; the steep tree-covered bluffs that crowded out the sky were simply there, another fact of life. "Your program over?"

"Yes, our program's over," Ro said, mocking his tone in turn. As she came out on the porch, her mother followed her out the door. Jerry listened to his wife's heavy steps, her thongs flopping on the old boards, felt her weight as she leaned on his shoulder and eased herself down on the stoop beside him. She reached over and took the Iron City.

"Sure. Make yourself at home," Jerry said.

"It's more my home than yours." Reina lifted the curls of thick black hair off her sweaty neck. With the skirt of her muumuu hiked up, the veins in her plump legs stood out blue against her olive skin. "You're never here."

"That's because I'm always working so you can live your life of luxury."

Reina puffed once like blowing away a pesky gnat. At times he could catch glimpses of the pretty Italian girl he had married their first year out of high school—his high school sweetheart, before he knew better; before he found out that he could talk to other girls, before he found out that other girls would talk to him—though it could be a stretch. It helped that time and gravity had been kind to her bazoomas; he still liked to catch a peek of them through the loose armholes among her underthings.

"Mom, did you hear what Mrs. Brioschki told her husband when he told her he has cancer? She told him, right to his face, 'Drop dead.'" Ro laughed.

"Ol' Fred's already died a thousand deaths, living with a wife like that," Jerry said.

"A husband like that," Reina said, handing him back the can, "deserves to die a thousand deaths." Jerry and Reina looked at each other.

"That's what she told him, when he told her he has cancer. 'Drop dead.'" Ro laughed all over again, standing behind her parents, as if she'd never heard it before.

Stephie lay down across the second step from the bottom, just below Jerry's and Reina's feet. She folded her hands across her boyish chest and closed her eyes; light and shadow, from the sunlight through the trees of heaven, worked back and forth across the little girl's face.

"You okay, dear?" Reina said to Stephie, not really looking at her.

"We could go on a picnic," Ro said.

"Who said you were going anyplace with us?" Jerry said.

"We're going to have a picnic right here," Reina said.

"You can't go anyplace without me," Ro said, ignoring what her mother said.

"I'd sure like to try," Jerry said.

"We'll have a cookout in the backyard," Reina said. "That'll make it special for your father. Like the Fourth of July or something."

"Well, the hell with you," Ro said, looking down on the top of Jerry's head, not letting it go. "I can always find something to do."

"Yeah, we got proof," Jerry said, nodding toward Stephie.

"You're rotten." Ro swatted him on the shoulder. Jerry reached for her, low and quick, but she dodged away, ran for the protection of the door. "Stephie, what are you doing down there?" she yelled from behind the screen, her forehead dented against it. "Get in here."

The little girl bent in the middle like a V, lifting her head and feet at the same time, to get herself up. As she passed between her grandparents, walking on her heels, Jerry palmed her ass, barely a handful. "How come you're no good, pumpkin?"

"I don't know," Stephie said, singsong, thinking about it.

Reina puffed air up over her face to cool herself, then leaned on Jerry's shoulder again—Jerry grunted under the weight—to help herself get up and follow them into the house. "Well, if we're going to have anything to eat later, I better get busy."

"Don't strain yourself," Jerry said, but it was wasted, she was already gone. The screen door banged behind her.

In the yard the tall grass stirred; the leaves of the lilac bush beside the house rattled. Jerry turned his face to the warm wind and, in a kind of toast to the day, raised the Iron City to his lips. Empty, of course. Oh well. He crimped the can in one hand like they did in the commercials on TV—a guy in a bar one night showed him the trick involved—and put it on the step between his feet. The breeze found the can and rocked it back and forth on its crease; Jerry folded his hands and hunkered over, resting his elbows on his thighs, staring down absently at the can between his legs. All in all he guessed he wasn't feeling too bad about things; as a matter of fact he guessed he was feeling pretty good. It felt okay to be home, to have a day off, with nothing particular to do, nothing particularly to get done, a little time for himself, a day of relaxation for the working stiff. Who said no rest for the wicked, ha ha. The can below the framework formed by his arms and legs seesawed back and forth, ticktocked with the breeze. Jerry picked it up abruptly to put an end to its little racket and carried it into the house.

Two

He was used to sleeping during the days now, what with his graveyard shift at the mill; add to that a couple of beers and he found himself getting drowsy. After another turn through the downstairs—there was a certain satisfaction that things weren't improving on the home front: Reina and Ro were in the kitchen arguing over whether or not there should be celery in the potato salad; in the living room there was a different game show on the TV but everyone was still green; who knew where Stephie had got to—he went into their bedroom at the back of the house and lay on top of the bed, thinking he'd only nap for ten minutes or so. He woke five hours later to the sound of female voices out the window and the smell of burgers on the grill.

In the kitchen, still dazed from sleep, he got himself an Iron City from the fridge and stepped out the back door.

"Well, look who decided to join the living," Ro said.

"Wasn't a choice. You talk loud enough to wake the dead."

Reina had the portable grill going midway up the backyard. Ro and Stephie were seated at the picnic table under the make-shift shelter at the back of the house. Along with another young woman Ro's age. A pretty blond girl in shorts and halter.

"Dad, you remember Julie Gumbowki?"

"Frankie's little girl? Nah, Julie? How're you doing? You were about this high the last time I saw you. Last time ol' Frank came back for a visit." He was fighting hard to wake up; he wished now he had taken time to splash some water on his face, make sure his hair was okay, that the upsweep in front was the way it should be. As much as a subterfuge as anything else, stalling for time to get his thoughts together, he leaned down and put his arm around her. Gave her a squeeze. She looked up at him with an uncertain smile. As if she wasn't sure what he was up to, but was curious, thought he was nice, was willing to play along. Jerry kept his arm around Julie as he stood beside her. Longer than necessary.

"You better watch out, Julie," Ro said. "I think my dad's up to something."

"He might *like* to be up to something," Reina said, turning the burgers on the grill. "But I can tell you I know for a fact that ol' Jer isn't up *for* anything."

Jerry tried to think of a comeback but the laughter rose up too strong against him and he kept quiet. He listened for a moment or so as Julie talked to the others, his arm still resting on her shoulders. She didn't seem to mind. But as soon as it seemed natural he eased away from her. Palmed Stephie's head to show he was just an affectionate kinda guy. He moved out on the grass and took the spatula away from Reina.

"Let a man do this."

"Let me know if you find one." Reina slapped him on the arm.

Jerry busied himself with serving the food, making sure everyone's beer glasses were filled, making sure he had a fresh can of Iron City at hand. He sat at the head of the table to eat, listening to the three women gossiping about the town—Ro said, "Did you hear what Mrs. Brioschki told her husband when he told her he has cancer?" Julie said, "Who's Mrs. Brioschki?"—about the changes to the town since Julie and her family moved to Texas. He tried to keep his eyes to himself, but he couldn't help notice that every time he chanced a look at Julie, at her breasts swelling her halter, he caught her looking back at him. And she would smile. But soon enough he grew bored and restless; he felt foolish sitting there listening to the three women, staring at the collection of dirty paper plates and crumpled napkins spread out in front of him, shooshing the occasional fly away from the relish jar and ketchup bottle and the top of his beer can. Definitely not the way he wanted to spend the afternoon on his day off. He stood up from the table—the three women looked his direction but kept on with their conversation—stretched, and carried his empty back into the house and got another beer from the fridge. Did the girl look disappointed when he left? Maybe so. Well, too bad. He went into the living room, reclaimed his recliner, and turned on the Pirates game. It took him ten minutes of up and down to fiddle with the controls to get the colors right again.

After several innings he dozed; he woke when he heard the women come in and go upstairs, still jabbering. The game was over, the commentators were doing a wrap-up but no one mentioned the final score. Now everything on the screen was tinted red. Jerry flipped himself up out of the chair and headed, a bit unsteady—he felt more drunk now than he had earlier, tipsy— out the back of the house to check the grill. It was only late afternoon but the day this close to the river was in early afterglow, the sun in this part of town already beyond the valley's hills. At the mill a Bessemer converter began its heat, rolling over in its berth, sending clouds of gray smoke flickering orange and yellow above the rooftops, cutting off the sky and shadowing the backyard. The warm breeze he encountered earlier in the day on his front porch moved in the branches of the dogwood tree in the vacant lot next door, played with loose strands of his hair. He pulled his shirttail free from inside his pants and lifted it up to feel the warm air on his skin; he rubbed his stomach as he moved tipsily through the half-light. The briquettes still glowed in the grill pan. He decided to dowse the thing with water and be done with it. Reina could deal with the grill tomorrow. Serve her right for leaving him with all the work. He turned back to the house to get the hose when he realized someone was sitting at the table in the shadows under the shelter. Watching him.

"Oh. Julie. Hey. Hiya."

He went over and stood under the edge of the shelter, reached up and took hold of the edge of the corrugated plastic sheeting he had rigged there as a roof, let his arm take his weight as if he were suspended there, swaying as if blown in the breeze.

"I walked right by you. Never saw you sitting there," Jerry said.

"I thought you were ignoring me," Julie said. She was sitting with her back to the house, her elbows on the table, a cigarette in one hand. A flicker of a smile coursed across her face and away.

"Not good ol' Jer," he said. He let go of the roof and tried a little bow—at your service—but it didn't work. He realized he still had his shirttail pulled up and was showing his stomach. He fuddled it back into place. Mumbled an apology. Everything he said seemed to come out in a sputter. He tried to laugh but that sputtered too. She continued to watch him with a look he thought somewhere between amusement and interest. Maybe the ol' Jerry charm was still working for him. Maybe she came out here just to see him.

"So what are you doing out here all by your lonesome?"

"I wanted a little air. It's been a long time since I saw the mill smoke fill up the sky. I tell people in Charlotte about it and they don't believe me."

Jerry looked at the sky the color of rust. He remembered how he greeted her earlier in the day. He moved farther inside the shelter, around the table on the pretext of joining her to watch the sky, to get a better look at what she was looking at. Stood beside her at the table. After a moment he placed his arm across her shoulders. He jostled her, trying to be playful. He could see right down between her breasts in their halter.

"So, how are you, pumpkin?"

"I'm fine. How are you?" She didn't move away from him, she didn't do anything. Just looked up at his face, watching him, the little smile still on her lips.

He squeezed her. Pulled her closer to him, so she was against his thigh.

"I'll bet I know why you came outside. You came out here to see ol' Jerry, didn't you?"

She didn't move away from him. Didn't lose the little smile. But as she looked up at him, she said, "You forget, ol' Jer. I was out here first."

He looked down at the young girl's face looking up at him. But now through his beery fog he couldn't tell if it was a smile or a smirk. Or something else entirely. He dropped his arm from around her shoulders and moved away from her. Almost pushed her away from him. He stood there swaying slightly for a moment. Glanced at her only once.

"'Scuse me. Forget that. Forget I said anything. I've got to go." He headed back into the house. Bounced lightly against the doorframe in passing.

In the house he ducked into the bathroom as he heard Reina and Ro come back downstairs. He heard the back screen door slam, Julie's voice join the other two. Would she tell his wife and daughter what happened? What did happen? He sat on the closed lid of the toilet. "You almost did it for yourself that time, didn't you, Jerry-boy?" When he heard the three women move toward the front of the house, Reina and Ro making their good-byes to Julie and thanking her for coming, he slipped out of the bathroom and into their bedroom.

He was sitting on the edge of the bed when Reina stuck her head in the door.

"What are you doing in here?"

Jerry waved the question away. "I didn't want to listen to all that girl talk."

Reina studied him a moment, then came over to him. Worked herself in between his legs. "I think you made an impression on Julie."

"Why? What did she say?"

"Nothing particular. A woman can tell, that's all." She ruffled his hair, leaned back to look at him. "You know, you're not all that bad-looking. For an old guy."

Jerry grunted.

She ruffled his hair again, pulled it slightly. This close she smelled of cigarettes, a whiff of mustard. There was something he had thought to tell her, but he couldn't remember now what it was. She took his head in her hands and guided his face between her breasts. He decided as long as she was offering he might as well take it.

". . . I would no think sheep could get away so fast," Duncan MacMurchie says, following the older grenadier corporal up a dry creek bed.

"What's the matter, laddie?" Hugh Campbell says, without looking back at him. Keeping his eyes on the woods around them on the hillside. "I thought you Clan Donalds knew all about sheep."

"I'm no Clan Donald. I'm Clan Kenzie. I told you that. And the only thing you Clan Campbells know about animals is how to steal them, and that's the way of it."

"Your head is full of wee beasties, Dunnie my treasure—and they're all dead. Och, let's no start this out here. Keep your mind on the wee'uns what's missing. And the Indians."

He didn't mean to offend the MacMurchie boy. He only meant to kid him a little, try to ease the tension a little. He should have known better than to try to make light with the one the other men called Black Duncan, or the Black Lad.

The truth is both men hate sheep, lost or otherwise. They are Highlanders. Sheep are Lowland animals, lairds not clan chieftains measure their wealth in sheep. There were sheep in the Highlands, of course, a few kept around the sod cottages and little townships, but women and children looked after sheep. These men are Highlanders, cattlemen. The lives of Highland men for centuries have centered around the short black shaggy longhorn cattle of the braes and glens. Herding cattle, and stealing cattle. It was bad enough in Bouquet's army that they all had to help herd the sheep along between the two columns on the line of march, taking the sheep with them into the wilderness so the army would have something to eat when they got there. (Both men have had their *fill of mutton by this time too.) Now they've been sent up here on the hillside to try to find a dozen or so of the animals that broke away as they forded the river. Poor filthy silly dumb skittery sheep.*

The two men continue up the dry creek bed, up the slope of a hill within the valley's hills. They are out of sight of the river now. The Indians call this place Valley of the Crows. A crow calls from someplace near the river, but there is no longer the sound of the drums or the shouts of the drovers or anything else of Bouquet's army. Even the insects aren't as numerous now, there is nothing around them but the trees, trees. The call of a warbler. (Is it really a warbler?) The two Highlanders, their Brown Bess muskets, bayonets attached, held at the ready, climb deeper into the forest. . . .

ALMOST A SHUTOUT

1969

"What a game! Jeez, it was almost a shutout!"

JD angled across the sidewalk and lashed out with an open palm at the head of a parking meter, jingling it to its innards. Then he hugged it, draped his elbow over its crown like leaning on an old friend. Manny and Middleton followed him out of the Blue Room.

"Don't give me that," Manny said. "You didn't think they could do it."

"I didn't say they couldn't," JD said. "I was afraid they couldn't, that's all."

"It's the same thing. You didn't think the Steelers could do it. You gotta believe."

"I believe."

"You gotta believe."

"I believe, I believe."

Manny put his hands in his jacket pockets and joined JD on the curb, keeping an eye on the few cars that were out in the late afternoon. Middleton sat on the fender of his car.

"I wonder if Tag still watches Steelers games," Middleton said.

"Why wouldn't he watch Steelers games?" Manny said.

"You know."

"No, I don't know."

"You know, having once played."

"So?" Manny said. Hands still in his jacket pockets, arms winged out at his sides, he pivoted his torso a couple times, then tilted left and right, a kind of stretch. "What difference would that make?"

"So, he might not want to watch Steelers games."

"I bet he watches the games," JD said, chewing on his toothpick. "Once a Steelers fan, always a Steelers fan. Steelers Nation."

"Yeah," Middleton said. "But you might not be so crazy to watch a Steelers game if you once played for the Oilers."

Two guys in a pickup truck came along the main street. Manny didn't recognize them but the bumper had a parking lot sticker from the mill so he gave an upward nod. The guy riding shotgun gave an upward nod in return. Manny adjusted his shoulders. He and JD wore the letterman-style jackets—wool bodies with vinyl sleeves, black and silver, Furnass Stokers colors—they earned in high school, half a dozen years earlier, each with his name in script over the heart; Middleton's no longer fit so he wore his United Steelworkers of America jacket.

"Tag never played for the Oilers. He tried out but he didn't make it," Manny said.

"He played on the practice squad for two years," Middleton said.

"That's what I said," Manny said. "He never played for the Oilers."

"He made it further than the rest of us," Middleton said.

"That's for sure," JD said.

"The practice squad isn't anything like playing a game," Manny said.

"What are you jawing about?" JD said to Manny. "You never even made it that far."

"I didn't have a scholarship to a big-name school like Tag, either. How could I make it?"

"You didn't have a scholarship because you weren't as good as Tag."

"You couldn't even make it in junior college," Middleton said.

"All I'm saying is," Manny said, "don't try to tell me Tag played for the Oilers. 'Cause he didn't."

JD, leaning at an angle against the meter, let his weight fall forward, his arm slipping off the top, as if he would spill out into the street, catching himself at the last second. After two successful self-saves, Manny faked a punch to his arm; JD juked and stumbled forward off the curb.

"Shit."

"Let's walk," Middleton said.

He lifted himself heavily off the fender—his car gave an audible sigh of relief—and started down the sidewalk. Manny joined him, and JD slow-dragged a few running steps to catch up. The main street was nearly deserted, the bars closed from the Sunday blue laws; the Blue Room always set up a TV in the restaurant section specially for the games. The three young men caught their reflections moving across the lighted display windows, the blackened interiors beyond; only JD acknowledged the vision, taking the opportunity to rake his hand back through his hair. All three lifted on the balls of their feet as they walked like teenage athletes. In six blocks, they covered the length of the downtown, to the top of the hill before the main drag dipped into the Lower End, marked by Saint Botolph's Church on one corner and Mikey's All-Niter on the other, crossed the street and headed back up the other side. Tin angels hanging from the light poles faced each other along the empty street tooting silent horns, the garlands already hung for Christmas stirred occasionally in the late autumn wind. The red lights flashed yellow warnings mainly to each other.

"Hey, was that Tag in that car?" JD said.

"Where?" Middleton said.

By now the car in question was a block away.

"You're seeing things," Manny said. "He's still in Houston."

"You've got Tag on the brain," Middleton said.

"Sure looked like him," JD said. "Maybe he's home for the weekend or something."

"Then he'd be heading back already," Manny said. "Besides, he would've let me know."

"Maybe he didn't. Let you know," JD said.

"Maybe he heard you were bad-mouthing him about his time with the Oilers," Middleton said.

"Funny guy," Manny said.

"Sure did look like him," JD said.

"He would've seen us. He would've stopped, or something. Honked," Manny said.

"Probably wasn't him," Middleton said. "No reason to come back to this place. Unless he had to."

"Maybe he had to," JD said. When the others looked at him, he shrugged. "Maybe his mom is sick or something. I'm just saying."

"How's he doing down there, anyway?" Middleton said. "Anybody hear from him?"

Manny shrugged.

"All of us could be heading for Houston," JD said. "If the mills close."

"Speak for yourself," Manny said. "I ain't going anywhere. And that's just bullshit, that the mills are going to close. The mills will be here forever."

"Tag always was the smart one," Middleton said. "In more ways than one."

"Yeah, where's he going to get a job like that around here?" JD said. "And that kind of money?"

"I heard Janet's expecting again," Middleton said.

"If she was your wife, wouldn't you be giving her as many babies as you could?"

"Mind your manners, son," Manny said. "That's Tag's wife you're talking about."

"I'm just saying," JD said

"Those are beautiful kids, to be sure," Middleton said.

"That's what I'm saying," JD said. "That's one beautiful woman."

"You wouldn't know the first thing to do with a woman like that," Manny said.

"But it sure would be fun learning my limitations," JD said, draping himself over Middleton, collapsing into soundless laughter.

"Here you go," Manny said, taking a rolled-up newspaper from a trash bin. He flexed his knees, ready to take the ball from center. He looked left and right, checking the defense, looking for one-to-one coverage, looking off the linebacker. "Blue seventy-nine . . . blue seventy-nine . . . Hut! Hut! . . . Hut!" He skittered backward as Middleton and JD headed down the sidewalk, Middleton as corner to JD's slot receiver. Manny scrambled away from the blitzing safety, out of the pocket as JD started a crossing route. The pass was wobbly and high and landed behind him in the gutter.

"Great pass," JD said.

"Shit, you were supposed to go long. No wonder Sonny always threw to Tag."

"No wonder you were always a linebacker," JD said.

Middleton retrieved the paper, faked a couple dribbles, and took a jump shot at the trash can. The paper hit the rim and pinwheeled to the sidewalk.

"And that's why we lost the state championship," Manny said.

"You would know, Ace," Middleton said.

The trio, each one with his hands deep in his jacket pockets, elbows winged, continued along the empty sidewalk.

They recrossed the street on the diagonal and were back at the Blue Room. It was getting dark now, the gray of the afternoon descending into evening; the streetlights flickered on, progressing one by one along the main drag. JD said he was on four-to-midnight this week, he'd see them Saturday; Middleton needed to get home to get ready for graveyard. Manny stood by himself on the curb for a while, then got in his Camaro and took another turn through town, scanning the radio for his songs, something by the Carpenters or Captain and Tennille. As he passed through the Lower End, on the off-chance, he stopped at Tag's house, a few blocks from the mill. At the end of the block, a few kids were shooting baskets at a hoop hung on the chain-link fence of the mill; beyond the fence a donkey engine shuttled a string of empty slag cars toward the blast furnace, waves of heat still rising from the white-hot ladles.

The grocery store at the corner of the building had been closed for years, since Tag's father died—was it ten years now? Manny found it hard to believe—but Manny went around to the side door and walked in without knocking. Several of Tag's sisters were curled in nightgowns on the sofa in the living room, watching TV; none seemed surprised to see him in their midst, but he couldn't tell if it was their meds or if they just weren't connecting tonight. Tag's older brother Bucky—one of the three or four who still lived at home—a janitor at the high school, in the blue work shirt and pants that he wore all the time nowadays, sat on the second-floor steps eating an open-faced peanut butter and jelly sandwich; he mouthed a happy greeting as Manny passed through, as if Manny were another of his siblings. In the kitchen Mrs. Taglianetti was busy making sandwiches for tomorrow's lunches; on the table eight or ten small paper bags clustered together open-mouthed; the slices of bread were splayed in front of

her like a deck of cards, the jars of peanut butter and jelly, may-
onnaise and mustard, canned tuna fish and potted meat lined up,
each container with its own knife. She was happy to see Manny,
as she always was, though she barely lifted her eyes from what
she was doing—"Would you like a sandwich? Oh, go ahead, have
a sandwich, *mangia, mangia!*"—and when he asked she said
Tom's last letter several months ago said he didn't think he'd
have time to make it home this year.

. . . The woods are colorful and bright. The fluffy mass of red and yellow leaves blocks out the sunlight but covers the hillside in light. Directly above the creek bed, there is a raggedy cleft of blue sky between the trees. The midday sun bears down on the two soldiers, the grenadier corporal leading the way, the private of light infantry in his shirtsleeves behind. A blue jay screeches from the lower branches of an oak tree. It hops from branch to branch as it works its way up the tree, a reoccurring flash of blue and white, then flies off to another tree and starts over again. A woodchuck pauses to look at the two men, sniff the air, then waddles on into some ferns, aware only that there's something different in the woods today. A crow, two crows, call from the other side of the valley.

There are a number of differences between the two men. The older man wears the grenadiers' tall miter-shaped bearskin hat, whereas Duncan MacMurchie wears an infantryman's blue wool bonnet. Hugh Campbell is tall, even for a grenadier—always the largest men in the regiment, the men who stand in the place of honor at the far ends of the battle lines, or stand behind the lines, ready to shore up any weakness or lead a charge, shock troops. Duncan MacMurchie is a tad shorter than the five-foot-seven average height for the Black Watch, but he is average height for a Highlander. Hugh Campbell has the fine yellowish-red hair of the Campbell men, long almost to his shoulders. His eyes are the blue of sunny skies, or at least that's what the doxies back at Fort Pitt tell him. Duncan MacMurchie's hair and eyes are dark brown, but that's not why they call him Black Duncan.

Hugh Campbell comes from a long line of Campbell men who have served in the Black Watch. He enlisted fifteen years earlier, when his clan chief, his ceann-cinnidh, wanted to show his continued loyalty to the English Crown. At the time, the Black Watch still had much the same feel about it as when it was formed a number of years earlier. Then only gentlemen's sons were chosen, the men were the fairest in all the Highlands, selected for their good looks and overall bearing as well as for their ability to fight, and even the privates had their own servants or gillies to carry their packs. Duncan MacMurchie comes from a family of drovers, wild nomadic barefoot people with no land of their own who eked out a living driving other men's cattle to market. After centuries of selling their services to whoever would pay the most, they had peripheral kinship ties with several clans. Recent generations swore their allegiance to the MacKenzies, but their loyalty didn't count much when their ceann-cinnidh decided he needed to thin out his tenants. Duncan MacMurchie was sold into service to the English Crown for ten guineas.

For all that, the two men have a few important things in common. Whether they know or would admit them. Among them: that neither one wants to be out here wandering around the woods looking for sheep. The still air carries a faint pungent acrid smell. There are only the sounds of the forest around them, the scuffing of their stiff brogues in the dust. The creek bed curves ahead of them. The two men stop. . . .

LARRY-BERRY

1978

There was a draft down around my feet, I could feel it. I couldn't seem to get the quilt the way I like it, with the bottom tucked in tight, there was still a leak somewhere. I tried to start over, tried to work the quilt down by lifting up my feet and pedaling so it would arrange itself around my socks, but I could still feel it, the cold air creeping up my legs, and finally I gave up trying.

Rita was in the bathroom with her two girls—they had been in there most of the afternoon. I could hear them chattering away, giggling to each other like a bunch of kids. It was Jackie's birthday—she was twenty-four; the other one, Bobbie, was only nineteen—and Rita used it as an excuse to invite them over for the day. And after all the trouble we had about her seeing them when we first got married, what could I say? It was the girl's birthday, and they are her daughters after all, and I guess she's got a right to see them, even if they are a pain in the old *dupa*. But I told her straight out, just don't expect me to ruin my day because of it, she could do what she wanted to do because I was going to do what I wanted to do, no matter who was here, and she understood that. So after lunch they all trooped into the bathroom and I rolled up on the floor with my blanket and pillows to watch the Penn State game.

But, you know, it's hard to ignore somebody you don't like. It's harder to ignore somebody you don't like than it is to pay attention to somebody you do like. Or at least that's the way it seems to me. Because all that girl Jackie has to do is walk into the room and she gets to me, I can feel it in my stomach. I don't even have to see her, I know when she's around. So while I was lying there watching the game, the bathroom door opened and closed, and of course you know who came down the hall and stood in the doorway. I didn't know what she wanted and I didn't want to find out. I could see her reflection in the television screen—for a moment there she was a dancing partner for the Nittany Lion—but I'd be damned if I was going to speak to her. Then I decided I'd be damned if I was going to speak to her first. Then I decided what the hell, I'd speak to her and get it over with.

"What're you doing in the bathroom?" I said to her image on the screen.

I could see her smile at her little triumph. "Nothing."

"You're sure making a lot of noise for doing nothing."

"Bobbie's trying out some different hairstyles on Mom."

"Great."

"Some of the stuff she's been learning at school."

"Great."

"You don't sound very excited."

"Great."

"Don't you want your wife to be beautiful?"

I let her wait a while. There was a young hotshot quarterback scrambling around the backfield, trying to win the game all by himself, and being chased by half the defensive line. But he finally got away. I still wouldn't look at her.

"It would take more than a couple weeks at beauty school to make any difference on Rita." I was proud of that one.

"You're awful," she giggled.

It is proof to me of God's infinite wisdom and justice that the girl not only acts like a pig but actually looks like one. Puffy cheeks, square nose, wet beady eyes. Even her body looks like an upright version of a porker's. To my way of thinking it is a perfect example of the order of the universe. What I've never understood is how she ever got married. Or how she left her husband for somebody else, and not the other way around. Or how she left number two for number three. Or why one, two, or three would ever want her in the first place. There is still a lot in this life that remains a mystery.

"Rita sent me out to see if you want anything." A referee cranked his arm like a propeller mounted on her chest.

"Nothing you could give me," I told her.

"You're terrible, Larry-berry."

"That's not what the girls tell me."

"What do the girls tell you?"

"They tell me I'm wonderful."

"Then they lied."

"You'll never know about it."

"I will if you show me."

A typical woman: she took insults for interest. When will I ever learn that women can't take a joke? When will I ever learn just to keep quiet? I watched her on the screen as she came across the room, a secret smile on her face; she stood right over me, I could hear her shoes making squishing noises on the rug, but I still wouldn't look at her.

"Don't you want to show me what makes you so wonderful?" she said, soft and sticky.

"Why would I want to show you anything?"

"You might like it."

"I might not either."

"You won't know if you won't try, Larry-berry."

"I never did like well-traveled highways."

"Depends on how good a driver you are."

"She-it, girl!" I said, and tried to burrow a little further into the quilt.

"Larry-berry, Larry-berry," she called in a little singsong voice, and put her foot on my shoulder and rocked me back and forth. I was afraid she'd lose her balance and fall on me and make me as one-sided as a nickel.

"Larry-berry your ass," I muttered from my covers.

"If that's the way you want it."

"You're all mouth."

"Like I said, if that's the way you want it."

"Get out of here, girl."

She laughed and rocked me a couple more times with her foot and I was afraid she was really going to squash me. But she finally gave me a little kick and went back to the bathroom. I heard the door open and close and the three of them laughing, and I thought it would be like her to tell her mother and sister what happened, the whole story, everything we said. I unraveled a little bit and just got the pillow where I like it when, sure enough, the door opened and the three of them came down the hall.

"Don't look, Larry-berry!" Rita shouted without coming into the room. "Don't look!"

"Wild horses couldn't make me look."

"I want it to be a surprise."

"It'll be a surprise, all right."

"Don't look, Larry-berry," Jackie said.

"Don't look, Larry-berry," Bobbie said.

I pulled the quilt up as far as it would go over my head.

"Promise you won't look?" Rita said.

"Why would I want to look at you?"

"Promise? Honest Injun? Boy Scout honor? Right hand up?"

"Right hand up your kazoo."

That pleased Rita; she and the girls giggled. On the screen I could see them peering around the edge of the door like the Three Stooges. They finally came into the room but stayed near the safety of the doorway.

"Jackie said you asked her to mess around. Is that true, Larry-berry?" Rita said.

"Yeah, sure. Hey Jackie, you want to mess around?"

"See? I told you," Jackie said.

The girl is a real pork chop. It was a good thing Rita took it as a compliment—there are definite advantages to marrying a woman who isn't too swift. She was standing between her two daughters, grinning like she'd just been named Mother of the Year. I couldn't make out that her hair was any different, partly because the camera was jumping around trying to cover a down-field punt, and partly because I couldn't remember what her hair looked like to begin with.

"You wouldn't play around on me, would you Larry-berry?" Rita said.

"I wouldn't tell you about it if I did," I said. Which was the truth.

"He wouldn't play around on me," Rita told her girls, "because he loves me."

A grunt on my part seemed sufficient.

"He looks like a log lying there," Jackie said.

"A log in a quilt," Bobbie said.

"I'll put a log in your quilt," I said and they loved it.

Rita pretended to slap at them. "Don't talk that way about Larry-berry. He's my husband."

"He still looks like a log in a quilt," Bobbie said.

"You say worse things about him than that," Jackie said.

"That's because he's my husband," Rita said proudly and they giggled some more.

"Go away, I want to watch the game," I said finally.

"I came out to ask if there's anything you want."

"I want you to go away."

"Are you hungry? I'll fix you a pizza burger if you want."

"I'll give you a pizza my mind if you don't get out of here."

"You're not hungry?"

"No."

"You want something to drink?"

"No."

"You want a kiss?"

"Ugh. You'll make me throw up."

"You want to make love?"

She and her girls stood there grinning back and forth at each other. I just let them stand there. Finally she got the idea and said, "Come on, let's leave Larry-berry alone." She baby-talked to them as she herded them out of the room and back to the bathroom. I could already tell how all this was going to end. She'd get herself all gussied up and then say It's a shame not to go out someplace. Then she'd ask if she could take them to the Holiday Inn out at the airport or someplace like that, and then she'd say she didn't have any money. The truth was, I didn't care if she went out or not. Matter of fact, I guess she should go out. I figured it would be nice for her to take her kids out and show them a good time. Of course I'd never tell her a thing like that.

I thought I'd finally get some peace and quiet, but a few minutes later the bathroom door opened and closed again and I was afraid they were coming back. But it was only Bobbie. I watched her on the screen go into the kitchen while the coach and trainers ran out on the field to help a downfield receiver who got clotheslined by the monster man. I thought she was taking an awfully long time in there, and I wasn't surprised when I saw her come quietly into the room and lean against the doorframe.

"Are you asleep, Larry-berry?" she said softly.

"Nah. What you want, kid?" I said, still watching her on the screen.

"I wondered if you'd like a Pepsi?"

"Sure, that'd be nice."

She hopped out of the room and appeared in a couple of minutes with a glass. She was still moving quietly though, she had taken off her shoes, and I realized she didn't want Rita or Jackie to hear what she was doing. I kept my head low and I could hear her moving behind me, but the next thing I know she's stepped over my head and was squatting down in front of me and I'm face-to-face with her toes.

They're cute toes. I've always liked her toes. They lift and wiggle and squirm like ten little puppies as she shifted her weight around, getting a coaster for the glass. I kept my head buried but she evidently wanted to show me something else, because as she squatted there she spread her legs so I could see under her skirt all the way up her thighs.

"There it is, Larry-berry."

"It certainly is."

"Is there anything else you'd like?"

"I'd like you to get out of the way."

"You're so cute, Larry-berry."

"Come on, you're blocking my view."

"Let me give you a kiss, Larry-berry."

All I really wanted to do was watch the game. But she put her arms around me and gave me a big hug and tried to kiss me on the cheek. I dodged her a couple times, long enough to get a glimpse of a terrific rollout by the quarterback, but the screen was blocked again by the flash of her quat. I ducked down under the blankets, but not too far, not so far that she couldn't find me and give me a big wet kiss on the lips. She's a good kid.

"Why don't you pick on someone your own size," I said. She put her head on my shoulder and her hair smelled nice.

"Smarty-pants," she said, not angry, and tucked me in.

"What happened to your boyfriend?"

"Oh, him? I got rid of him."

"Did you give him back his ring?"

"Absolutely not."

"But you were engaged."

"He gave it to me for Christmas, so I figure it was a present."

"But you can't wear it now."

"Who wants to wear it? I can sell it."

"Nice girl."

"I'd be a nice girl to you."

By this time, she had me tucked in so well that the quilt was like a straitjacket and I could hardly move. She took my head in her hands and was getting ready to do a number on my mouth when Rita and Jackie came out of the bathroom.

"What are you doing to my little girl, Larry-berry?" Rita said. Bobbie dropped my head back on the pillow and stood up. Her toes waved good-bye.

"Larry-berry gave me a kiss," Bobbie said and stepped back over my head. I watched her on the screen rejoin the others.

"He wouldn't give me a kiss," Rita said.

"He wouldn't let me get him a Pepsi," Jackie said.

"Why'd you let her, Larry-berry?" Rita said.

"Because Bobbie's better-looking," I said.

I was still wrapped up tight and it seemed like too much trouble to try to get out. On the screen I could see Rita had added lipstick since her last appearance but it only made her look like she'd been sucking blood. She stuck out her lower lip and put on her little-girl whine.

"But she doesn't love you the way I love you, Larry-berry." She knelt down behind me and gave me a big squeeze, tucking in the last little corner of the blanket around my head. I was snug as a bug in a rug, free of care as a bear in his lair, warm as a worm in a womb.

She began to roll me back and forth like a giant rolling pin, singing, "Larry-berry, who'll you marry, Larry-berry, won't you marry me."

"Stop it, you're making me sick."

"Why wouldn't you let me get you anything?"

"Because I've got enough trouble."

"Last night you called me the maid."

"Well, that's what you are."

"I'm not your maid. I'm your wife."

"Quit reminding me."

She straightened up a little and beat a tattoo up and down my back, then grinned at her daughters. In the warped reflection of the tube, she looked like a painted Mau Mau drumming messages in the jungle.

"I'll get you anything you want."

"I've got everything I want."

"That's because you've got me."

"Who wants you?"

"You want me."

"No, I'm stuck with you."

"You love me, you know that."

She beat another message on her husband-drum.

"Hey, that hurts!"

"You're in love with me, aren't you, Larry-berry?"

"No way."

"Come on, say you're in love with me."

"I'm in love, but not with you."

She rapped me with a knuckle on the upper arm that really hurt. I gave a holler and made like I was going to grab her but she jumped up and they all scurried out the door.

"Don't look! Don't look!" they shouted as they ran down the hall. I was glad they left, I was wrapped so tightly that it was going to take some doing to get out of it and I didn't want to look foolish.

"I'll show you in a minute, Larry-berry," Rita called from the bathroom.

"I'll show you, you ever hit me like that again."

They giggled. "You wait there," Jackie and Bobbie said in chorus.

"I'll wait, all right," I said, and turned back to the television. They had messed around so long, the first half was over already and a band was pumping up and down the field, the kids with impossibly high steps making formations I couldn't understand. And it occurred to me that waiting was one of the best things I did, it seemed like I had spent all my life waiting for a better job or better friends, more money or a prettier woman. It occurred to me that I had been waiting for something so long that I wasn't even sure now what that something was.

The screen showed a line of little honeys in cowgirl outfits, cute little bolero jackets trimmed with fringe that wiggled with the movements of their breasts, short pleated skirts that flew up around their incredibly full thighs and their satin panties. Down the hall the bathroom door opened one last time and Jackie and Bobbie sang, "Ta-da!" Across my tiny image of the cowgirls, Rita came into the room with her too-red lips and too-puffy hair, her hectic, frantic eyes and cocker spaniel smile.

"You can look now, Larry-berry."

I sighed and rolled over in my cocoon to look at this woman my wife, knowing that whatever it was it was all I was going to get.

. . . Ahead is an area of deep shade. Hemlocks and pines and tangles of laurel—but mostly hemlocks—crowd both sides of the creek bed, tunnel-like. The branches of the thick evergreens interlace among themselves into layers of nets. Inside it seems dark as night, impenetrable, impossible to see through. The Shades of Death. That was what such areas were known as on Bouquet's march from Carlisle to Fort Pitt. The worst one was on Laurel Hill, when the whole army gripped their muskets, bayonets fixed, expecting any moment to hear the shrieks of Indians. It was said that Braddock's army in '55 was massacred in another Shades of Death.

Hugh Campbell squats, studies the dust of the creek bed. There's fresh dung, and sheep tracks leading right into the dark trees. Duncan MacMurchie, standing behind him, begins to hum a pipe tune, "Flowers of the Forest."

"Hush, lad. None of that."

"Afraid, Clan Campbell?"

Hugh spits into the dust, stands up again. Looks the younger man in the eye. "There's no use tempting Providence by humming a funeral dirge, is there now?"

"Aye. I did no think. But are you afraid?"

Hugh doesn't answer. He hefts his musket in his hands a couple times, as if weighing it anew, nods for the other to follow him. If he ever stopped to think about it, he might find he is afraid. The thing is, he doesn't think about it. The feeling other men call fear has been part of him for so long that it almost seems natural to him, as familiar to him as being hungry or tired. It is like an old friend, indistinguishable from or the same as the feeling of being ready to fight again. The curious mixture of alertness and ease. Terror and excitement. Rage and peace. A rush of emotion that makes him forget every other consideration. It is the time, those moments when he is ready to kill, that he feels the most alive.

What bothers him is that Duncan MacMurchie asked him about it. They say the Black Lad is a seer. That something happened to him at Bushy Run, so that now he has the second sight. That he can see other worlds. That he can see the future, a man's destiny. Has Black Duncan seen something now? Something about Hugh Campbell?

It is cool inside as they enter the evergreens. At once they are assailed by bugs. Flies nip at Hugh's ears, buzz at his eyes. The smell of the hemlocks is bitter, choking. As they continue into the deep shade, he takes his dirk and holds it in his left hand, under the stock of his musket. The blade pointed toward him, ready to slash with his backhand. The way he was taught his ancestors held a dirk under their studded bullhide targes in the glens of Argyll. At Bannockburn in the 1300s. At Culloden. . . .

AUGIE'S KWIK DOG

1982

"This is exciting, you know?" Augie DeAngelus said, looking out the front window.

"And another thing. I don't have to put antifreeze in it," Homer said to Augie's back. When Augie didn't say anything, he looked at Ada behind the counter. "You know that? I don't have to put any antifreeze in it neither."

"If you say so, Homer." Ada walked on, carrying dirty dishes to the back.

"This is really great. I've never seen a snowstorm when it was starting before," Augie said.

"That's because you never looked," Homer said. "That's because you always stay safe indoors and don't get out on the street."

"Augie's not a big one for opening his eyes," Ada leaned out from the doorway in the back, for a moment her face brightening. "Ever."

"Uh-oh," Homer said. "Sounds like a revolution to me. Sounds like feminism raising its ugly head."

"Ada wouldn't do that." Augie looked back over his shoulder, his little-boy's smile, the smile of a happy eight-year-old, taking over his face.

"And another thing," Homer said and chewed air. "I don't have to get no insurance for it neither."

Augie's Kwik Dog was a small place, half a dozen tables and half a dozen stools along a counter, tucked into an old storefront on a steeply angled side street, down the hill from the main street and a few blocks from the mills and factories along the river—the perfect location, or so it seemed when they first leased it, to get both shoppers from upstreet and workmen on their breaks. The day Augie and Ada opened the Kwik Dog six months earlier, after Augie lost his job at the mill and decided it would be fun to run a restaurant, was the first day Augie ever cooked for anyone besides an occasional meal at home. He learned many wondrous things that first day, such as that cooking oil can catch on fire and that eggs cooked too long turn out like white shoe leather and that there are a lot of hard-to-please people in the world. Yes, many wondrous things.

"Boy, the top of the hills over there just disappeared! Watch out, the snow's on its way."

Ada, wiping off the tabletops, getting ready for the lunch crowd—such as it was—looked past Augie out the large front window. Beyond the rooftops of the buildings stacked down the street toward the river, the snow advanced as a dim line along the crest of the valley; the bare trees faded to gray then were erased completely. The man, the man. The man would drive her crazy. Or he'd let her work herself to death in a hot dog shop, whichever came first.

"Well, I guess I better get on my rounds," Homer said, getting up from the stool at the counter and putting on his sandwich boards again. He was a stocky old man, perhaps sixty-five or more, his face barbed with white growth, dressed in layers of clothes he made himself from old sacks and castoffs he picked up around town. When he passed, Ada winced; Homer smelled of trash bins and burlap and soggy wool. The sandwich boards were actually pieces of cardboard he wanted to keep with him to sleep under in case he couldn't find any other place when night came. Over the years the message of the boards had evolved from biblical phrases and prophecies of doom (which nobody read) to a long rambling complaint that he didn't get his mail (the truth being that there was no mail for him to get) to a walking bulletin board where people taped up announcements and listed items for sale and Homer posted the lottery numbers and his own thoughts for the day (people around town understood what was meant when somebody said "I read it on Homer"). His thought for today was NEVER RATTLE A RATTLESNAKE, though by this time of the morning he couldn't remember why he thought it was significant. Sandwiched up, he tunked softly between the tables, knocked between the chairs, to stand beside Augie at the window.

"Look at it this way. If anything goes wrong with it, I just push it back to the lot and gets me another one. Bet you can't do that with yours."

They looked out at the vehicle in question. It was a supermarket cart, tied to a parking meter at the curb, filled with what Homer called his collectibles, things he found around town— pieces of scrap metal, discarded umbrellas, a garbage bag full of bottles and another one of recyclable cans, hubcaps, an old suitcase filled with his personal items.

"And I don't have none of the other problems you folks do neither. I don't have to clean it or flush it out or nothing."

"I don't have to do that stuff either." Augie turned and looked at his wife, his face bunched up with merriment. He wore the outfit he bought himself when he first opened the place, the blue and white hickory-striped pants, the white double-breasted chef's jacket; his front was stained with meat juice and spaghetti sauce, as messy as a butcher's. "I've got Ada. 'Course, sometimes I have to knock her around a little, to keep her in line. Right, Ada?"

He took a poke at her as she passed. Ada glared at him but she knew he would hit her for real if she pushed too far—he had in the past—and she continued on to the back. The man, the man. When they decided to open the place, she thought of getting herself a nice uniform too; she saw herself in frills and a lace apron laughing with men in business suits, but jeans were good enough now. She was a tiny woman, her hips ballooned out from having three children in a row, her black hair in a functional Dutch boy, her face still pockmarked from her teenage years; when she was behind the counter, men looked at her ass, but not a second time. She gathered up the few breakfast receipts and dumped them in a cigar box under the register; she'd have to do all that later, they had to get ready for lunch.

The snow started in the street, ticked against the window. After Homer left, Augie came back between the tables. "Did you hear what Homer said? He said he wants to get snow treads for his cart. That Homer."

On the walls were Ada's hand-lettered signs for STEAK SALAD $2.45, MEATBALL SANDWICH $1.50, WEDDING SOUP $.90, JOHNNY MARZETTI $2.25 PLUS SALAD—testaments that Augie had learned to do more than hot dogs. Augie's little-boy face beamed at her. She thought they would have had such beautiful children, such beautiful boys, if they looked like him; instead their three boys looked like her, pinched-faced. As she adjusted the pies in the display case she looked at her hands: red and chapped as a boxer's. When she picked up the kids at night at his or her mother's, the kids didn't want to go home. She couldn't blame them.

"I'll bet you never thought when we opened this place that it'd turn out like a social club, did you? People like Homer just stopping by because they like it. Did you?"

Augie looked around proudly. He loved the enormous old Fox stove and the long-handled spatulas; he loved his orange juice machine and the eight-hole toaster (he never knew they made one so big). Pretty soon they might need a larger coffee machine, and he had learned the importance of keeping one pan just for omelets. He grinned at Ada and walked over and put his arm around her.

"Don't start it, Augie."

"I wasn't starting anything, Ada. I just thought."

"I told you then and I'm telling you now. Not again. Don't even start it."

"I won't," he said. "I won't."

Ada went on back to finish the dishes, her face drawn into an expression that her husband in times past mistook for a smile—she guessed she told him, she guessed she put him in his place. Augie was a little boy again, though not a happy one now; he was pouty, and later perhaps dangerous. He idled over to the stove and scraped the griddle a couple times, keeping an eye on the front. Outside the large front window, the snow gusted in the street, the buildings stepped up from the river began to disappear, dissolve into a million pieces. Later on he'd have to have a talk with Ada, get a few things straightened out. But for now he guessed he'd have to be satisfied, waiting for the lunch crowd to come see him.

. . . It is dark within the hemlocks. Not as if it were nighttime exactly, it is more the not-quite-dark, not-quite-light of an eclipse. There could be a hundred Indians around them, they would never see them in here. Never know they are here until it is too late. For that matter, they could walk right by the missing sheep too. Hugh Campbell leads the way through the Shades of Death, wishing he had a tankard of ale right about now. He glances back over his shoulder. In his white linen shirtsleeves, Duncan MacMurchie coming along behind him appears to glow in the murky light. Hugh Campbell wishes he were back at Fort Pitt, at Suckie Sly's alehouse in the Lower Town with a doxie sitting on his lap.

At Bushy Run, after the battle, they found Duncan Mac-Murchie wandering in the woods. The day before, the Indians had boiled down through the trees at the front of the relief column when it was only twenty miles from Fort Pitt. After the Indians, in their crescent-shaped attack, began to attack the rear of the column as well, Bouquet withdrew his troops to a nearby hill. They fought the rest of the day, in the heat and humidity of August, circled on the hilltop without fresh water. The Indians would prod the circle and then fade away, prod and fade away, never allowing the Highlanders the chance to get at them. The next morning, in desperation, Bouquet came up with a plan to draw the Indians into the circle and give the Highlanders that chance.

Duncan MacMurchie was in the company of light infantry who pretended to panic and flee back into the circle. And when the Indians poured in after them, Hugh Campbell was in the company of grenadiers who along with the light infantry circled around out of sight behind a spur of the hill and charged the Indians from the rear. Charged them with their muskets and broadswords as they screamed their own clan battle cries and ended up chasing the Indians two miles through the woods. When they came upon Duncan MacMurchie afterward, he was walking along touching the trees, his bloodstained broadsword in his hand, a distant look in his eyes. He didn't seem to recognize any of his mates, and all he talked about were the crows, a crow. They figured he must be a seer, that he had been given the second sight sometime during the battle. Black Duncan. The Black Lad.

In the Highlands, a man kept an eye on the man beside him in the line of battle, to compare himself with the other, to see how he measured up. But Hugh Campbell wonders who there is to compare himself with now. Out here in the middle of nowhere, clambering around the wilderness with a half-crazed lad in tow. It is one of a number of sad thoughts that have plagued him lately. On the march from Fort Pitt he began to wonder for the first time what he was doing here at all. The answers he could come up with did nothing to ease his mind. He had joined in service to the Crown to impress a clan chieftain who acted more like an Englishman than a Scot. To bring glory to an English king who acted more like a German. To defend the lands and honor of the English who considered Scotland a hole for vermin. A nursery for soldiers. Poor silly dumb stupid Hugh, is what he thinks. Is he afraid? He doesn't really know what "afraid" means at this point. But he is very tired. Tired of it all. The government in Philadelphia said they weren't going to allow any more whites to settle here this far west. That once Bouquet's army got things quieted down, they would leave this part of the country for the Indians. But Hugh knows what will happen. The settlers will come anyway—who could stop them? Come here to make new lives for themselves. Hugh Campbell is thinking that maybe he'd like to make a new life for himself. To settle down with a bonnie lass, build himself a home, raise a wee bairn or two. Have things. To not fight anymore. In the darkness of the hemlocks, despite telling

Black Duncan earlier to keep quiet, he sings to himself, in an undertone, in Gaelic,

> *If I was as I used to be,*
> *Among the hills,*
> *I would no more mount guard*
> *As long as I lived. . . .*

SMITTY'S SERVICE

1979

Smitty wasn't sure he heard what he thought he heard until he stopped his own hammering on the tailpipe. Then he stood underneath the car, his arms weighted down with the hammer and chisel, his face wedged in between the frame and the brake lines, and listened for a moment: there was the radio on the workbench, tuned to a late-night music station from up in Pittsburgh; there was the compressor pumping away in the back room; there was the ringing in his ears. And yes, there was a tapping, *tap-tap-tap*. Smitty ducked out from under the rack, away from the trouble light hanging from the axle beside his head, and squinted, blinked into the gloom. Blood-red patches of afterimage slid down the dark walls of the garage around him. There was somebody outside, tapping carefully with one knuckle on a pane of the overhead doors.

As Smitty came over, the figure outside stepped back, looked up, expecting the door to lift. Instead, Smitty unlatched the small access door within the larger door and swung it open.

"Come on in," he said and headed back to his work.

The man outside stared at the awkward door a moment, then eased through sideways, being careful not to touch or brush up against anything. Smitty sized up his visitor—nope, this certainly didn't appear to be anyone who was going to try to rob him, catch him after hours; in this part of town you had to think about such things—and ducked back underneath the car. The man was around Smitty's age, a little older perhaps, late forties or early fifties, pencil-thin and good-looking, with a close-cropped beard as narrow as a chin strap and a touch of gray around the temples, dressed in a poplin windbreaker, chinos, and loafers. Probably from Highlands or Sewickley or some rich place like that—a lawyer maybe, or business executive—and obviously embarrassed, uneasy, out of his element.

"What can I do for you?" Smitty said, shifting the trouble light to a hole in the frame.

The man, his hands in the pockets of his chinos, leaned carefully into the circle of light beneath the car. "Muffler?"

Smitty looked at him and nodded.

"I tried to change one once when I was a kid. Took me the better part of a week and I still had to call in every friend I knew to help me with it."

Smitty didn't doubt it in the least.

"That can be a real chore."

"You looking for work?" Smitty said.

The guy was flustered. "No. No, actually I'm having some difficulty with my car. . . ."

Smitty stared up into the undercarriage, waiting for the rest of the story. He was not a big man though the slate-gray coveralls he always wore—wore so much of the time that people around town sometimes had trouble recognizing him without them—made him look thicker than he was. In his class in high school there had been two Bob Smiths, Big Bob Smith and Little Bob Smith: he was Little Bob Smith, though in all fairness nearly everyone in school was short compared to Big Bob. (He had seen Big Bob recently at their class reunion, the first time Big Bob had made it back in thirty years—he had flown up for the occasion from Orlando where he was an architect. Everyone wanted snapshots of the two Bob Smiths together. Big Bob looked great, tan and healthy and obviously rolling in money; and standing next to him for the photographs, Little Bob still looked little.) His wedge-shaped nose and the general construction of his face, along with his preference for wearing coveralls—which also started in high school where he spent most of his time in auto shop—gave him the teenage nickname "Muskrat"; he was really glad as he got older that people started calling him "Smitty." His customers usually didn't include the Highlands and Sewickley types—Smitty knew that if the guy had a choice he would probably drive ten miles out of his way to go someplace else—but he wasn't going to turn him away; owning a service station in a mill town, he was grateful for any business he could get.

"I don't know what's the matter with it."

"Wanna give me a clue?"

The guy looked at him to see if he was joking. Smitty nodded a couple times, jacked his eyebrows, to encourage him. The guy smiled, a little sheepish.

"Well, it runs okay downhill. But it conks out going up."

Smitty gave the stubborn tailpipe one last whack, and ducked out again from under the car. "You got it outside?"

"What?"

"Your liver."

"What?"

Smitty loved it when he could get somebody like that. "Your car. Is your car outside?"

The guy kept a careful distance away from him, as if afraid the dirt on Smitty's coveralls was contagious. "No. It's out there on the road toward Mars, past Mingo Junction. I told you, it conks out going up hills."

"How'd you get all the way in here?"

"I started walking and a couple guys in a pickup stopped and brought me in. They were real nice about it."

Smitty wondered just how nice, seeing as how they left him at a station on a back street where all the lights were out and a sign on the door said CLOSED. He had seen cars stripped during hunting season in less than half an hour.

"What kind of car is it?"

"Porsche."

"I think we better get out there," Smitty smiled wryly. "While there's still something left of it."

"Oh, there's somebody with it. . . ." As soon as he said it, the guy got a sick look on his face.

"Somebody?"

"Well . . . a woman."

"You mean you left a woman all alone in a car way out there. . . ?"

"At the time it seemed like . . . the thing to do."

"Yeah, well, the thing for us to do right now is to get the hell out there as soon as we can," Smitty said as he bustled over to the sink to wash his hands.

He led the way to his tow truck, parked outside next to the building. It was an old Dodge Power Wagon that Smitty had resurrected from a junkyard; he had even painted it himself with a brush, fire-engine red, along with the runny black lettering on the doors, SMITTY'S SERVICE WE DO ANYTHING. The service station was on the back side of town on Twenty-Fourth Street Extension, tucked in among a few run-down houses at the foot of the valley's hills. It was almost eleven o'clock. With his passenger holding on for dear life, Smitty peeled rubber across the driveway, bumping over the curb; their headlights danced crazily over the railroad embankment across the street—a pair of red eyes, a raccoon, stared at them from the weeds and tall grass. Gunning the truck past the culvert leading to Downie Hill Road, Smitty wound it out along Walnut Bottom Run, along the base of the valley.

Conversation in the old truck was impossible once they were rolling, the grind of the transmission almost as loud as the growl of the engine, but that was okay with Smitty; most of the time he rode by himself and he liked it that way best anyway. He put his arm out the window and punched the wind, his sleeve whipping like a flag; the night air slipped up his arm and ballooned his coveralls around him until he felt twice normal size. He also liked it best when he was Smitty-to-the-rescue. The guy beside him sat gingerly on the edge of the seat, among the rags and old coffee cups and doughnut wrappers; his feet were wedged in between some gears for a differential and Smitty's jumper cables, his hands tucked between his legs, all scrunched into himself. Smitty looked over at him and grinned friendly-like and gave him the thumbs-up. Tonight he even liked his rider, his new friend from Highlands. The guy was probably all right, once you got to know him; he couldn't help it if he didn't know what he was doing. Smitty hummed a little tune to himself, watching the white lines streak toward him like tracers.

Once he skirted Onagona Memorial Hospital and cleared the city limits on Indian Camp Road, Smitty gave the Power Wagon its head. Barreling through the countryside, the country roads he used to race on when he was a teenager, the truck's caged headlights swept over the scraggy brush and dry leaves that reached out from the shoulders. It was desolate country, strip mines and scratchy farms, the hill people who lived out this way backward and unfriendly. He turned on the CB, both hoping and afraid he'd hear police calls—Uh, Dispatch, this is Car Two, you better get an ambulance out here right away, we got a lady in pretty bad shape and a stripped Porsche—but there was only a jeep party trying to link up toward Indian Camp, coon hunters most likely. A few miles past the old mushroom mine, his high beams picked out the car sitting on the shoulder on the other side of the road. As he swung across the white line and pulled up in front of the disabled car, the woman inside looked frightened, then relieved, and climbed out to meet them.

"You okay?" the guy said, hurrying out of the cab and along the berm to her.

"I'm glad you got here. A car with a couple men stopped a little while ago and said they wanted to help, but I didn't like the looks of them and wouldn't unlock the door. They finally gave up and went away but I was afraid they might come back."

"Well, you'll be okay now," Smitty said, sauntering up to join the couple standing in the glare of his truck's headlights, his hands wedged jauntily into his coverall pockets.

"And this is our knight in shining armor," the woman said, looking at him and smiling.

"Honey, this guy isn't—"

"We're lucky to find anybody to come all the way out here at this time of night to help a lady in distress, aren't we?"

"Yes, but I don't think we want—" the guy started to say but she cut him off.

"Stop fretting, Craig. I just know we're in good hands now," she said and patted Smitty's arm.

"Yeah, well," Smitty said, blushing and shuffling his feet in the gravel. He looked off into the dark trees beside the road. "I guess I'll, ah . . . have a look." He pointed to the car and walked on past them.

She wasn't at all what Smitty expected, though he couldn't have said exactly what that was. She was a tall elegant attractive woman, with bobbed blond hair and blue eyes; she was wearing the same kind of chinos and loafers the guy wore, with a sweater tied by the arms around her shoulders. Smitty had no idea how old she was—she could be his age, she could be a dozen years younger—regardless she seemed younger than Craig. She reminded Smitty of the girls at his class reunion, girls who were women now, the great-looking ones who looked even better as they got a little older but still had traces of the girl they used to be right below the surface. As Smitty squeezed in behind the wheel of the Porsche and turned over the starter a few times, he tried not to look at the couple talking together in the glare of the truck's headlights, the light flaring off their silhouettes like starbursts.

Craig left the woman and came over to the open car door. "You don't usually work on foreign cars, do you?"

"Nope." Smitty turned it over again. The engine finally caught; he listened to it for a moment, revved it a couple times, then turned it off again.

"I think you better just tow us to a dealership. These cars are very delicate, you know."

"I don't usually work on them," Smitty said, climbing out from behind the wheel, "because most people around Furnass can't afford a car like this. But that doesn't mean I don't know *how* to work on them."

"What's going on, Craig?" the woman joined them.

"I'll tow it into my place and see if I can get you going tonight. Otherwise, I'll take it to Sewickley tomorrow, that's the closest dealer." Smitty shrugged inside his skin of coveralls, it was up to them.

Craig shook his head. "I don't think you should play around with—"

The woman put her hand on Craig's arm, then leaned toward Smitty. "That sounds fine to me."

"Mickie, I don't think—"

"Craig, I think I'm the one to make this decision." She smiled doubly hard at Smitty, tight-lipped. "And I think what this gentleman says makes a lot of sense."

Smitty, feeling pretty good about things, got in his truck and backed it into position with much engine growling and grinding of gears. From the bed he unloaded the carriage wheels and hoisted the Porsche; he covered the nose of the car with an old rug to protect the finish. Then he tried to clean out the cab of the truck a little, sweeping the garbage out onto the shoulder and dumping the junk in the back so there would be room for all three of them.

"You mustn't go to any trouble," Mickie said, coming over and standing behind him in the open door.

"Oh, no trouble. No trouble at all." He realized the rag he was using to wipe off the seat was an old pair of his underpants; he wadded them up and threw them into the bushes behind her, hoping she hadn't seen what they were. Before he could say or do anything else, she climbed up into the cab and plopped herself down in the middle of the seat, folding her hands in her lap and giving a sharp nod to signify an end to the matter.

"This will be splendid. Simply splendid. I've never ridden in a big truck like this before. I'm sure it'll be quite an experience."

Smitty and Craig looked at each other. Smitty walked around the front of the vehicle, cutting into the beam from each headlight in turn, to get in behind the wheel.

As the three of them got settled on the seat, Smitty wished he had put on a pair of clean coveralls before coming out here tonight; he wondered if she could smell his socks. He started to reach for the gearshift and stopped: the floor lever crooked up between her legs and was going to travel into some questionable areas before they got out of the lower gears. She sensed something was wrong and looked at him quizzically, then laughed at his dilemma.

"Yes, you do have a bit of a problem there, don't you?" she laughed again. "But it'll be all right, I've got slacks on. And besides, I know I can trust you. I feel like we're old friends already."

Smitty wasn't so sure he could trust himself—Please God, don't let my hand slip, please don't let me miss a gear—but he laughed too, and carefully got the lever into first and eased the truck forward, off the shoulder and up over the edge onto the pavement. The car dangling behind them surged forward a couple times—he was afraid it was going to bump them despite his being careful—but then it settled down as they got going and gradually picked up speed.

"This is very exciting," she said toward his ear. "An adventure."

"It's a little hard to talk sometimes," he grinned at her. Smitty leaned forward to include Craig in his comment, but the guy was staring straight ahead, a glum look on his face. Smitty thought To hell with him.

"And you're a very good driver too," she shouted at him.

Smitty wrinkled his muskrat nose and shook his head. "Nah. I'm just along for the ride, same as you. Everything else is up to Jezie here."

"Jezie?"

"Jezebel. That's the truck."

She raised her eyebrows and looked at him questioningly.

"I named her for my ex-wife."

"Your wife was named Jezebel?"

"No, her name was Betty. But she acted like Jezebel."

She laughed silently above the roar of the engine, looking around at the night.

"She took off with a bartender from Alum Rock, about six years ago, best thing that ever happened to me," Smitty went on, hoping she'd laugh some more. "There's one main difference between my ex and this truck. I love this truck."

"Your wife didn't know a good thing when she had it," Mickie shouted toward his ear. "Jezie here wouldn't be anything without the man driving her."

Smitty's spirits soared. She was right: it was like they were old friends. It was like he was talking to one of those great-looking girls at his class reunion, Cathy Rutkowski or Sue Sentelli or somebody, somebody he had known a long time and could kid around with and who didn't get him all mixed up—it was even better, because none of those great-looking girls in his high school class ever had anything to do with him, then or now. Mickie wanted to know all about the gears; after he showed her how, she did the shifting while he worked the clutch. They growled along the country roads, the woman leaning against him on curves or when she spread her legs further to downshift; he could smell her perfume above the smells of gasoline and motor oil and his own musty clothes. He didn't want the trip to end, he wanted the night to go on forever.

Soon enough, though, they were coming down Cemetery Hill outside of Furnass again, the old Dodge racking off against the black hills, crackling like a slow machine gun, the Porsche slung behind nudging them like a reminder, a bad thought, down through the night toward the lights of Furnass, the streetlights winking through the black trees, the black patches in the shapes of the blast furnace and smokestacks and factory buildings marking the mills along the river, the buildings outlined with pinpoints of light like clusters of stars, the smoke and steam lifting around them flickering orange and yellow, then sinking down below the treetops until the lights of the town and the mills were obliterated by the black shapes of the trees around them, into the town itself. When he got to his dark service station he parked in front of the garage doors and climbed out. He never thought about it, he assumed the woman would get out the other side, but she called to him, "Here," from his side and held out her hands to him. After he helped her down, she laughed gaily and reset her hair with a toss of her head.

"How long is it going to take you?" Craig said, coming around the truck.

Smitty considered slugging him, on general principles, but told them he didn't think it would take very long, that he'd know right away if there was anything he could do to fix it. He suggested they wait at the bar at the corner, the D&G; they could get a drink or something to eat—but to make sure that it was Don doing the cooking, if it was his wife they'd be better off hungry.

"Some of the local lore, huh?" Mickie chuckled. Then she cocked her head at him and smiled. "And will you come over and join us when you're through?"

"Yeah, as soon as I know the situation with your car," Smitty said. "I might have a beer or something. If I eat anything this late it'll talk to me all night."

She chuckled again but Craig stood there looking worried and offended by the world. What's the matter, Craig-baby, Smitty thought, afraid I'm crowding your territory? After asking again where to find the bar, Mickie took Craig's arm and guided him across the dark apron, their heads huddled together as they discussed something. As Smitty lowered the Porsche to the ground, she looked back once and gave a little wave; Smitty waved back. They passed under a streetlight, her blond hair glowing like an acetylene flame when the mix isn't right. Then the couple was gone in the shadows, heading toward the neon lights of the D&G at the end of the block.

Smitty got his metric tools and his timing light and his *Guide to Foreign Car Repair* and set to work. It was the timing, as he had thought. He didn't bother pushing the car inside the garage, he tinkered with the settings there in the driveway; his adjustment wasn't perfect by any means but it was good enough to get the couple where they had to go tonight. When he was satisfied with it, he washed his hands, first with soap and then with Ajax and then with soap again, digging at the grease under his finger-nails with his penknife; he plastered his hair down with cold water and the flat of his hand, and put on a clean pair of coveralls from the bundle just back from the uniform and rag service. Fixed up as best he could, he locked the place and sauntered, his arms crooked out from the pockets of the coveralls, whistling a happy little nameless tune, flipping out his feet as he walked, down to the D&G.

It was an Insulbrick-covered frame house—actually the siding was made to look like stonework, not brick—that was converted during World War II into a café and tavern; it still looked like a private home with a couple electric beer signs in the front window. Inside, the lights were always on so the serious drinkers could see what they were doing. The place was homey, with the bar where the living room used to be, and mismatched tables and chairs scattered through the other downstairs rooms; the stairway to the second floor had been removed to make more room, but the last few treads still hung in the air leading to the gaping dark hole in the ceiling. Earlier in the evening when the shifts changed, it took both Don and Gloria at the bar to line up all the shots-and-beers for the hands coming and going, but now at one in the morning there were only a few men left at the bar. The couple was sitting with their heads together in the corner of a back room down the hall. Before he joined them, Smitty stopped at the bar. Gloria, a plump dark-haired woman in her sixties, with Don's tattered wool sweater around her shoulders, was already drawing him an Iron City.

Where'd you pick up those two?"

"Out Indian Camp Road. Had some trouble with their Porsche."

He felt proud of himself, expansive, and protective of his charges. Smitty took his first couple of swallows—he always liked best that first rush of an icy beer, that cold spike going down his throat, almost painful—as he looked around the place. He was ready to tell the tale of Smitty-to-the-rescue, but he knew from experience that Gloria wasn't an appreciative audience. From here the couple was mostly hidden by the doorframe; he could only see their arms spoked on the tabletop, a fragment of a chino pant leg and a penny loafer underneath.

"That's not all the trouble they had, I guess."

"Don't know what you mean."

"They asked to use the phone. You know, I couldn't help but hear, a small place like this. . . ."

"Oh sure, Gloria," Smitty laughed, chewed air a couple times. "Well, I expect they had a babysitter to call or somebody, tell 'em they were okay. But I got their car running—"

"Babysitter my foot. Husbands and wives, you mean."

Smitty only looked at her.

Gloria looked sly; she leaned forward, cradling her heavy breasts on the countertop. "You didn't think those two was married, did you?"

"Yeah, well, I guess, why else. . . ?"

"They was out doing their hanky-panky, that's why else. And then they got stuck with car trouble and had to call their married folk and try to explain why they're so late. She did pretty good— that's her car incidentally, you know that? But the way he hemmed and hawed, something about some old friend out in Ohio, I wouldn't've believed him either. There's going to be hell to pay when they get home, all right."

Smitty didn't say anything. He stood holding his beer, his other hand wedged deep in his coveralls, staring through the archway toward the room where they were.

"Don't get me wrong," Gloria said, straightening up and waddling down the bar to wash out a glass. "I don't begrudge nobody nothing. Let 'em do whatever they want. Just don't go putting on airs about it, you know? I mean they didn't fool me for a minute, coming in here all la-di-da. You know what she said to me when I served them? She said it was 'splendid.' She said they were feeling better already because of my 'magnificent smile.' Can you imagine me making anyone feel better because of my 'magnificent smile'?"

Smitty couldn't imagine anything at the moment. His thoughts were a jumble, he didn't know what to think.

Gloria laughed like a loud puff. "Can you imagine me making old Don feel better because of my 'magnificent smile'? The only time I ever made him feel better was when I was on my back with my legs waving in the air. . . ."

Smitty left her laughing to herself and carried what was left of his beer across the hall to the back room where the couple was sitting. Mickie brightened up as soon as he rounded the corner but Craig continued to look miserable.

"You got it fixed, didn't you. I can tell by the look on your face."

"Yeah, it'll get you . . . where you got to go. You better get somebody else to look at it though, as soon—"

"That's wonderful, simply wonderful. See, Craig, I told you our knight in shining armor here would save us."

Craig looked at him with a look of dread on his face, as if he could already see the real dragons waiting for him over the next horizon. "How much do we owe you?"

"Oh, I guess thirty-five for the tow," Smitty said, unable to look at anything but the floor. "And another five for the adjustment. . . ."

Craig pulled out a slim wallet from his back pocket and put two twenties on a beer stain on the checkered tablecloth, but Mickie wouldn't hear of it. "Don't be ridiculous, you foolish man." Craig looked as if he didn't know which one she was referring to; but Smitty knew. "It's got to be more than that, all the wonderful things you've done for us. Give him another twenty, Craig. He's worth it."

Craig did what he was told and sank back into his visions. Smitty was confused, all he wanted to do was get out of there, but Mickie reached across the table and took the money and squeezed it into his hand.

"Thank you, thank you so very much. You can't know what your help and kindness has meant to us tonight . . ." She was smiling but her eyes were frantic, she seemed almost hysterical. Smitty couldn't bear to look at her; he pulled his hand away and mumbled good-bye and left.

He walked quickly down the dark street back to his station. Inside he locked the door behind him and stood in the darkness of the empty bay for a few moments, until his breath started to come back to him. The money was still in his hand. He unwadded the bills and looked at them in the light coming through the glass doors from the streetlight across the street; he smoothed the wrinkles out of them and folded them neatly and stuck them in the pocket of his coveralls. Then with his hands in his pockets he shifted the coveralls around a bit, worked his neck in a circle to get rid of the crick, settled himself within the coveralls again.

The car he was working on earlier was still up in the air on the rack. He turned on the trouble light again underneath the car, turned on the radio again on the workbench; the compressor in the back room started up on its own, chugging comfortably in the darkness. On the wall above the radio was his collection of tool calendars, the large color photographs of girls in bikinis and work boots holding impact wrenches and grease guns, but Smitty didn't look at them now. He ducked back under the car again and found his hammer and chisel and took a tentative swing at the frozen tailpipe again, then began to hammer hammer hammer. He didn't hear the car start up outside in the driveway, and when the headlights flashed across the overhead doors as they pulled away into the night, he paused only a moment.

. . . Crow, crow,
Your mother's awa',
For powder and lead
To shoot you all dead. . . .

Duncan MacMurchie sings to himself. Ahead of him the figure of Hugh Campbell moves through the gloom. A dark figure moving through the dark evergreens. He thinks the older man must be crazy, to care this much about a few sheep. He thinks this grenadier corporal will get them both killed. As he follows along behind, a large black fly lands on his hand as he grips his musket. The fly stomps its feet, pivots to another angle, sets down its tongue to taste the man, then flies off again. Bitter, wee buggie? Duncan listens for the crows back down in the valley, close to the river. Crow, crow, have you any songs for me?

Not that this was something new. Being in the army, he soon enough got it through his head, meant that he was always being led (or driven) someplace where there was the chance that he'd be killed. And to kill, of course. Nor did he think it particularly unjust. That was what an army did; that was the way of it then, was it no? That was why they trained, that was the reason for the discipline, the endless drill. Wheel left, wheel right. Form column, form square. The regulation twenty-five motions to load and fire a musket. Seven motions to fix bayonets. Front rank, stand fast as you are. Shoulder your firelocks . . . Rear rank close . . . March. There were always drummers to beat the commands, there were always officers to beat the men who didn't obey. It was discipline that held them together when the Indians attacked at Bushy Run, discipline that held them together on the hilltop. Discipline that kept them from panicking when his company feigned a retreat to draw the Indians closer. Of course it was something else when they turned around and hiked their kilts up around their groins and chased the Indians through the woods. That was Highlanders being Highlanders.

Here in the wilderness now, there is only this grenadier corporal in front of him. He does not trust this Campbell. All his centuries-bred clan hatreds and suspicions are alive again. It was Campbells who massacred their hosts, the MacDonalds, at Glencoe. It was Campbells who ambushed and cut down the already beaten Camerons at Culloden, then murdered and raped all through the Highlands. It was said in ancient times the Campbells hoisted the babes of their captives on the points of their broadswords, then shook their swords in the air till the babes rattled down to the hilts. (Or was that somebody else, the MacDonalds of the Isles?) He could kill this Campbell and have done with it. Not that he wants to, but he could. It plays on his mind. Such thoughts play often on his mind since Bushy Run. He knows the others think he has the second sight since that day, that he sees ghosts and bogles. It is just as well. Just as easy.

They are coming to the end of the hemlocks. The dry creek bed leads on up the hillside, into more open forest. Hugh Campbell turns around to him and grins; they've made it. Duncan MacMurchie says nothing, does not smile. He listens for the song of the crows coming from behind them, from the floor of the valley along the river. Singing to himself,

> *The crows killed the kitten O*
> *The crows killed the kitten O,*
> *The muckle cat sat down and wept*
> *At the back of Johnnie's housie O. . . .*

FURNASS FOUNDRY & FORGE

1963

The two men in their mid-twenties were up to their ankles in leaves. Red and yellow leaves leveled the uneven terrain of the yard into a single multicolored mass. Overhead there were more leaves, layers upon layers of red and yellow (and brown too) leaves on the branches of the trees in the yards of the little houses, in the woods on the steep bluffs that mounted behind the houses—layers upon layers of leaves that would fall soon enough to join those on the ground and be either swept up or blown away or simply rot where they fell with the snows and rains of winter. It could have been a postcard scene of a picturesque New England autumn except for the mill town across the river, the steel mills and factories on the opposite bank. The two men looked into the open hood of the pickup truck beside the house.

"I'm getting spark but it won't turn over."

"Must be the fuel system."

"I guess. Or maybe the plugs are fouled."

"It'd still turn over."

"Yeah. Maybe."

The smaller of the two—a crimped-cheeked young man in baggy gray work clothes and a red bandana tied as a headband to keep his long stringy hair out of his face—reached in under the hood of the old truck and checked for the eighth or maybe the tenth time whether the wires on the distributor were tight, whether the coil was connected. Then Phil slumped over the curve of the fender, his chin on his forearm, one foot resting on the other, and stared at the engine.

On the broken walk in front of the house, a four-year-old boy rode his big-wheel tricycle slowly back and forth over the lumpy and crevassed concrete. As he kept an eye on the two men, the little boy made puttering engine noises between his lips— *Bwrarmmmm! Bwrarmmmm!*—a sound that came very close to that of a strawberry; in the process, he slobbered over himself, spittle trailing down his chin onto his gray hooded sweat shirt. The larger of the two men, Rocco, his hands stuck in the pockets of his Sons of Allehela jacket, worked his shoulders, trotted in place, then bounced on his toes a few times, crunching in the leaves, as if invigorated by the chill in the air. Then he peered over Phil's shoulder, looking sympathetic and concerned. The two men stared at the engine a long time, as if waiting for it to tell them something, to make a pronouncement.

"Carol take the Ford?" Rocco said.

"Yeah," Phil said. "She doesn't get off till late today. I have to take the kid over to her mother's." He didn't say the rest of it, the rest of what he was thinking.

"I'd let you have mine, you know, but. . . ."

"That's okay. I got to get this one fixed." For the eighth or maybe the tenth time, Phil jiggled the battery cables—no, that couldn't be it, he had spark, but what could it be? There was no reason to get excited, no reason to worry, there was still plenty of time. "Did you hear anything yet?"

"Nah. I heard they called a few guys back last week. But then somebody else said they're going to shut the mill down completely in a couple of months, so I don't know. I don't have to worry for a while yet, I'm still getting my benefits."

There were two rows of small frame houses—they weren't really what could be called city blocks—facing the river, the first row with long backyards stretched up the slope until they became one large vacant lot, the second row with the backs of the houses hard against the steep wooded hillside, in a nook in the valley's wall before the Allehela River joined the Ohio ten miles downstream from Pittsburgh. It was called Westview, not because the view of the houses was toward the west (it was actually east) but because the two rows of houses were what you viewed when you looked west across the Allehela from Furnass (if you looked hard enough, if you happened to notice at all). The workers from the Furnass Boatyard once lived here, while the boatyard itself was still operating, from the mid-1800s, when the yard turned out some of the best stern-wheelers on the river, until after the turn of the twentieth century. At that time it was a tight-knit community of like-minded souls, but the boatyard couldn't keep up with the times—namely, the transition from river packets to tugs—and the bridge from Furnass, which once terminated here, was taken out to make way for the tall concrete viaduct of the Ohio River Boulevard across the end of the valley. Now the area was more isolated than ever, with only one way in or out, a long roundabout route that circled down from the boulevard and doubled back upon itself along an oiled dirt road under the viaduct; and there was a general feeling about the place, fostered mainly by those who lived in the main part of town across the river, that no one would choose to live here if they could help it.

As the two men stared at the dead pickup, traffic thrummed across the viaduct two hundred feet over their heads; there was the continual sound of tires singing on the pavement, the repeated clank of the expansion joints and grates, the occasional rattle of loose parts as a car hit a pothole. Then across the water came the ringing of church bells, the noon whistles from the mills and factories, from the Furnass Foundry & Forge where he worked. Phil looked across the river at the town. He wondered what she would be doing now. It would be noon at the restaurant where his wife worked, she would be busier than ever with all the people on their lunch hour, screaming for their coffee, for dessert, Check, Miss! She would be bustling up and down the aisle and behind the counter in her squeaky white shoes, her arms stacked with plates. A breeze stirred the leaves of the sycamores and maples in the yard. The little boy rolled slowly, one revolution forward, one revolution backward, watching the men. Phil took a crescent wrench from his toolbox on the ground; he leaned under the hood again to loosen the lines to the fuel filter.

"Breeze feels good," Rocco said unconvincingly, and then shivered in spite of himself. He twisted his torso halfheartedly back and forth a couple times; he had put on forty pounds since he played football in high school half a dozen years earlier, his face had gone doughy. "Did you hear about the guy last night over in Alum Rock? Walked into some bar and started blasting away with a shotgun. I didn't hear how many he got."

Phil shook his head; yeah, he'd heard. "The world's going crazy," he said, leaning farther inside the hood. He squiggled in over the fender until he was half-inside the engine compartment; his legs stuck straight out as if the truck were trying to make a meal of him. Who would she be talking to now? There would be guys along the counter, groups of guys in the booths, businessmen and construction workers on their lunch hour and guys between their shifts at the mill; guys leaning on their elbows, drinking their coffee, watching her, watching her ass, talking about her among themselves—Look at that, would you? Shit, I'd like to get into that. Hi Carol, how's it going?—while she smiled at them, made little jokes with them, talked herself out so that by the time she got home she wouldn't have anything to say to him, her smile worn-out so that all she looked was tired, so tired she didn't want to move, so busy during her days that she probably never had the chance to think of him even if she wanted to. He worked faster than he should, faster than he had to, jerky, fumbling; the wrench kept slipping off the connections. He skinned his knuckles; the wounds blossomed through the oil and dirt on his hands—he tried sucking at the skinned places but the blood kept coming back so he tried to ignore them—the blood dripping down onto where he worked. Despite the cool breeze, he was sweating; it flowed into his eyes like tears going the wrong direction, blinding him.

"And those people at that day care center? Who'd want to do a thing like that to a little girl?"

Phil reached over to put a collar fitting on top of the radiator so he wouldn't lose it; but either it rolled off or his hand bumped it or the damned thing jumped off of its own accord—whichever, the tiny brass ring disappeared into the leaves in front of the truck.

"Shit! Mother—"

"I got it," Rocco said. He came over and bent down and carefully removed some of the leaves until he came to the piece of metal. As he reached for it, the ring slid down between more leaves, then slid deeper, always just out of sight. Phil leaned out from under the hood to watch. Rocco removed the leaves one by one until he came to bare earth; the collar rested among some dead grass. He handed it back to Phil with a look on his face as if he'd uncovered a great mystery. Phil stuck it in the pocket of his work shirt and wiggled back inside the gaping hood.

"*Bwrarmmmm!*" roared the little boy on the front walk. He peddled furiously backward several feet, bumping over the broken cement, miniature chasms and cliffs.

From the house next door came a girl's voice screaming obscenities. A teenage girl burst out onto the front porch, slammed the screen door behind her, and whirled around to push against it, holding it closed. The screen bumped a couple times, pushed from inside the house by someone trying to get out; first the girl held the door straight-armed, then she leaned her shoulder against it. When she saw the two men in the yard she lowered her voice and said something to whoever was inside, her head inclined toward the screen as to a lover; she laughed and slapped at the screen flat-handed and ran across the porch and down the steps. The door popped open and a teenage boy, in his bare feet and wearing only jeans, his hairless chest as pale as a slug, ran out on the porch after her; when he saw the two men, he padded back inside. The girl was dressed in a cheerleader uniform—a silver sweater with the emblem of a black megaphone and the words FURNASS STOKERS spread across her breasts, a full black skirt with silver pleats that flashed when she walked. She angled across the yard to pass close to the men, kicking the leaves, a defiant smile on her face.

"You got a mouth on you, girl," Rocco said.

"He asked for it," the girl said.

"I'll bet that's not all he asked for," Rocco said.

The girl ran at him, shuffling through the leaves, her lips pressed tight with concentration; she was trying hard not to laugh, trying hard not to seem too pleased. She punched him half a dozen times on the upper arm.

"Ow, ow, ow, ow, ow, ow," Rocco said, his hands in his pockets again, turning away but not too far away. The little boy stopped pedaling and watched wide-eyed; Phil, lying on top of the engine, looked out from under the upraised hood as though from inside a cave. As the girl kicked on toward the street, Rocco called after her.

"Where you going all dressed up? That the way Hunkies go to church?"

The girl turned around and walked backward, giving her dark hair a shake. "You dumb dago, it isn't Sunday. We got a pep rally this afternoon. Wanna come and help me cheer?"

"You come back here, girl. I'll give you something to cheer about."

The girl stuck out her tongue, sneering and happy at the same time, and got in her family's old Buick. As she drove away in a cloud of blue-gray exhaust and pinging gravel, she tootled her fingers at them.

"She's a real piece of work," Rocco said, shifting his shoulders inside his jacket.

Phil didn't bother to look up as he kept working; he got himself distracted rechecking the wires and connections—for the ninth or was it the tenth time?—but now he was attacking the fuel filter again. "The whole family's like that. You know what'd happened to us if we'd ever talked that way?"

Rocco grunted.

The filter was in the shadows between the engine and the fender wall, awkward to get at; he couldn't see what he was doing, he could only go by feel. His arms ached with the stretching and he stopped for a moment, rested his cheek on the shoulder of his greasy work shirt, breathing in the smells of oil and cloth. Across the river the town was stacked layer upon layer halfway up the slope of the valley. Along the main street was the building where his wife was at this very minute, talking to someone else; at the foot of the slope, among the mills and factories close to the river—less than a mile from where he was but more than three miles from any way he could get to them—were the redbrick buildings of the Furnass Foundry & Forge, the brick shed where he spent most of his nights, where he worked by himself off in a corner, only a few shaded light bulbs shining down through the cave-like building, the echoes of his radio blaring rock and roll reverberating until the songs became only more noise, where he ground fins and imperfections from the racks of castings, the grinder in his hands shooting comet tails of sparks up into the darkness.

Things hadn't turned out at all the way he thought they would, the way he wanted them to. When he was in high school he loved Carol so much, and she loved him. He would meet her after school and walk her to work, meet her after work and walk her home; they couldn't be together enough. At night they parked out at Indian Camp or Berry's Run and imagined what it would be like to be married—always together, always in love and loving, they could hardly wait to graduate and make it come true. Now here they were; he hardly ever saw her. They passed only occasionally between the end of one's job and the start of the other's, handing the kid back and forth; the only time they talked was to argue about what they couldn't afford this time. What happened to all those other feelings? Where did everything go? He plunged his hands back into the dark beside the engine again.

He finished disconnecting the line from the tank and, keeping his finger over the end of the line so the gas wouldn't run out, worked the fuel filter loose. He held the glass bowl to the light: it was clean: there was a little sediment in the bottom but nothing that could block the entire system. So what the hell could it be? He wiped his forehead on the greasy arm of his shirt and set to work putting the filter back on again. He just got it in place and the connections to the lines started when behind him there was a scream. The little boy had backed his big wheel off the edge of the walk and was stuck in the leaves.

"You can get yourself out of there," Phil yelled at him over his shoulder.

The child started to cry. Phil made sure the lines were connected enough to hold them, then pushed himself up and slithered back out from the under the hood and over the fender and started toward the child, across the yard through the leaves, the wrench still in his hand. The little boy recognized the look on his daddy's face and quickly climbed off the toy and pushed it back up on the walk and climbed on again, whimpering only a little, his dirty face streaked with tears. Phil stopped and watched to make sure the boy was settled, his breath coming in catches; the little boy pedaled slowly, one revolution forward, one back, his head down and his eyes fixed on the yellow plastic handlebars.

A phone rang in a house on the other street, the sound drifting faintly over the yards and vacant lots. "Must be mine, shit," Rocco said, too anxious. He started off in a heavy trot, hands still in his jacket pockets, calling back over his shoulder, "You need anything?"

Phil shook his head but Rocco didn't see him. He ran on, pumping his shoulders, elbows angled out, plowing through the leaves, up through the long backyard and across the dirt street toward his house.

Across the river, a train of ore cars crawled from under the viaduct and started through the S-curves along the Allehela, tracing the riverbank around Furnass, beginning the long grade up the valley, a hundred identical ore cars, empty, the throb of the diesels filling the valley, pulsing in his ears. As Phil bent under the hood again, a leaf landed on the fender across from him; it scraped like a claw across the metal and off the edge and down with the others. If it wasn't the plugs and it wasn't the spark and it wasn't a clogged line, then what the goddamn hell was it?

He had worked on cars all his life, he was good at it—it was one of the few things he knew he was good at. He had never doubted before that he could figure out what was wrong with an engine, that was the fun of working on cars; he always knew that if he worked at a problem long enough he'd eventually figure out what was wrong and fix it. But today he was starting to get scared, almost panicky. He leaned down into the compartment to finish tightening the connections on the fuel filter but he twisted one the wrong way and loosened it instead; the connection separated. As he struggled to attach the line again he knocked the filter out of position and lost the fitting completely and there was gasoline all over his hands, numbingly cold, as he groped around trying to find things. His hands were shaky, he was getting frantic; there was gasoline running over everything and he couldn't see what he was doing and he couldn't feel where things were and he couldn't get it all back together—he didn't know what he was going to do, he had to get this thing fixed, he had to be able to get to his job, there wasn't anything else for him now, he had to, he had to.

. . . *Out of the hemlocks, the forest opens up around them. The tracks they are following climb a shallow embankment out of the old creek bed, heading off into the trees. The two men, momentarily side by side, start up the bank. Off to the left, there's an Indian standing beside an outcropping of rock.*

Hugh Campbell turns quickly, drops to one knee as he swings his musket around. Duncan MacMurchie tries to swing his musket around too. But he's on loose footing on the little slope and he's off-balance and falls on his face and slides back down the bank again. There's nobody beside the rocks now. Nothing to indicate there ever was.

Hugh Campbell stands, breathing heavily for a moment, bewildered. As he begins to relax again, he looks down at the figure sprawled in the dust.

"Aye laddie, and who is it you're going to fight lying down there? Is it the worms then?"

"I thought there was somebody over by those rocks."

"Och, well. And a murderous savage behind every tree too, I suppose." Hugh climbs the few feet to the top of the bank and looks around, to make sure what he said isn't true.

Duncan gets up and brushes himself off, scampers up the embankment after him, resetting his bonnet on his head. "I did see something beside those rocks. And you saw it too, and that's the truth of it."

Yes, he saw something. Or thought he did. But he doesn't want to agitate the Black Lad any more than he already is. Any more than they both are. He opens his tin-plated canteen and takes a drink. The rum-flavored water helps calm him down a little more. It's not strong enough to make him drunk certainly, but it gives him pleasant memories. He laughs a little, gently.

"*Poor wee beasties. Here we go to all this trouble to find them and bring them back. And all so we can drive them on into the wilderness and kill them ourselves to feed our bellies. 'Tis a pity.*"

"*And who do you speak of, Campbell, and who do you pity? Is it the sheep, or is it the King's soldiers who die like sheep?*"

"*Aye Dunnie, my darling, there's too much black in you, d'you hear me?*"

"*I hear you, and I see you too. I see you covered in blood, Clan Campbell, and it's your own. I see you carried like a sheep on the shoulders of the slaughterman. I see you with your spirit draining from you, son of Argyll, and I see the other soldier-sheep following behind.*"

Hugh stares into the other's eyes. Crazy lad. Hugh doesn't believe him for a moment. He puts his canteen away, spits into the dust and fallen leaves. But if it is true, let Death come. Death will find it has a fight on its hands, the same as anyone else who tries to take him on. "Cruachan," *Hugh says, softly but intense, the ancient battle cry of the Campbells. With his bayonet he pricks the head from an ironweed plant and walks on again, into the open trees.*

"*Tullochard,*" *Duncan says. The battle cry of the MacKenzies. And falls in once again behind him. . . .*

ANYWAY

One

"Make up your mind, Ronnie," Myrna said.

The boy looked at his mother and grinned sheepishly; when that didn't work, he pumped his shoulders and looked down at the shoes on his feet. Steven, two years older than Ron, slumped in a chair, almost parallel to the floor.

"Come on, squirt," Steven said. "Take 'em and let's get out of here."

Vince sat across from them, by himself. He couldn't blame the boy for not wanting them; they were the ugliest shoes he had ever seen: two-tone grape-and-tan running shoes, with swirly designs on them to signify motion. Still, the boy had to learn. Ronnie rocked back and forth, watching the shoes in the floor-level mirror; then he walked over to the display and looked forlornly at the pair he really wanted, the professional-style basketball shoes.

"Do you think they'll get some my size later?" the boy asked his mother.

"Honey, they don't make them in your size," Myrna said. "You heard the man. Your feet are too narrow."

The boy moaned a little. Vince stood up, a signal, and the boy looked helplessly at his mother.

"Take them off then," Myrna said, getting up too. "I'll try to run you up to Pittsburgh next week. Maybe we can find what you want there."

"Why can't he just take those?" Vince said. He straightened out her imitation fur collar.

"Because he doesn't like them and they'll sit in his closet while he goes on wearing his ratty old tennis shoes. He's like his father."

She tucked her coat around herself a little tighter and smiled at him, knowingly; she seemed happy, happier than he'd seen her in a long while, and he wondered what pleased her so much. She touched him on the arm with the flat of her hand before turning away, but then her smile was to herself.

"Come on, boys. Your father's got to get going."

She made the explanations to the salesman, and Vince held the door as they filed out. They stood for a moment to one side of the crowded mall, out of the flow of traffic, as they looked around. Steven and Ronnie began trading punches on the arm, each one harder than the last.

"What else is there?" Vince said.

"That's about it," Myrna said. "Unless you need some more thermal underwear for work."

Vince shook his head. "I've got enough for now."

Myrna, a twinkle in her eye, sang, a bit off-key, "You've got my love to keep you warm."

Their eyes met, and he said to her silently Don't start again. She smiled, without meaning it this time, and turned to the boys; the exchange of punches had grown to the hurting stage, and they both seemed glad when she broke it up and sent them on ahead down the mall. As they started to walk back toward the outside door, she took his arm and the bad moment passed.

As they strolled through the crowds of after-Thanksgiving shoppers, the stores freshly decorated for the coming holiday season, he felt he was happy too, happy to be with his wife and kids.

Or if not happy, satisfied, content; he wondered why he couldn't always feel this way, wondered where the good feeling went sometimes. Outside the sky was gray and lifeless, the day still undecided as to what it was going to do, though the wind pressed over the acres of parking lots. They broke into a stiff-legged run across the black asphalt, laughing at themselves as they crowded into the cab of the pickup, four across, Myrna scrunched up tight against him. As he started the engine, a pretty dark-haired girl in knee-high boots climbed out of her Firebird in the row in front of them, her skirt pushed halfway up her thighs; Vince took it as an achievement that once he looked at her, he looked away, that he didn't look at her again. And as if she read his mind, Myrna took his arm, claiming him for her own, as they watched their breaths clouding over the windshield.

Two

She had gone to a lot of trouble for the dinner; she didn't want to give him just leftovers, turkey sandwiches; she wanted to make it special. There was wedding soup, and rigatoni and meatballs, with a piece of beef cooked in the sauce for him alone, then roast chicken, and salad.

"Oof, I won't have to eat for a week," he said, patting his belly.

"I'm trying to fatten you up so other women won't look at you."

He looked at her: Don't start again. But she didn't say any more as she cut him a piece of angel food cake marbled with Jell-O, his favorite.

The boys spread out on the floor in the living room to watch the Pitt game. After she redd the table, she sat across from him as they finished their coffee.

"I wanted to make it special for you. Because you have to go in when everyone else has a holiday."

"Not everybody has off. There's still a skeleton crew. I told you that."

"I know," Myrna said, smoothing the wrinkles from the table-cloth. "I just wish you didn't have to go in at all. So we could spend some time together. And for a double shift. It's not fair."

"I told you, Myrna. Tatasio's taking off to visit his daughter in Jersey. I told him I'd keep an eye on his crew on graveyard. As long as I was going to be there anyway."

"It's just that you're working a lot of extra time in the last few months. And it doesn't seem you're making that much more money for all your trouble."

"There's talk there's going to be more layoffs. There's even talk they're going to close the Tube Mill, like they're talking about closing the whole Allehela Works. Pack it up and send it off to India or someplace. I have to show I'm someone they can count on. That's why I thought I should go in."

"You mean you didn't have to? Not even for your shift?"

"You want Christmas, don't you? What can I do?" Christ, what was he thinking, telling her that?

She nodded. Looked in the living room at the boys on the floor. Turned her coffee cup ninety degrees in its saucer, then back again.

"I have to take the work when I can get it."

"I just wish you didn't have to work so much . . . such long hours."

"Christ, Myrna. We've been through this. You want the boys to go to college, don't you? You don't want them to end up like me, do you?"

She turned her cup ninety degrees and back again. "I don't think you turned out so bad."

Don't start, Myrna. Don't start again. Please. "I have to go get ready."

Three

Over the sound of the water running in the sink, he heard her footsteps come up the steps from downstairs, go into their bedroom. He finished washing his face, combing his hair, making her wait a bit to acknowledge her presence, before he went back to the bedroom. She was sitting on the edge of the bed, swinging her legs, a bright new look on her face, the look she got when she was being playful, chewing a wad of imaginary gum.

"Hiya, mister."

Vince grunted; he wouldn't look at her as he got a handkerchief from the chest of drawers and put it in one pocket, scooped his loose change into his palm and put it in another pocket, put his wallet in a rear pocket.

"You're new in town, ain'tcha?" She pretended to chew her gum like a hick, openmouthed.

"Just passin' through."

"Ya wouldn't have room in one of your pockets for li'l ol' me, wouldcha, huh, mister?"

"Nope, 'fraid not." He still didn't want to look at her; he looked around the room to make sure he had everything.

"Well then," she smiled. "Suppose I told you I had room in li'l ol' me for big ol' you?"

He was wondering what he did with his keys when it dawned on him what she said. He looked at her surprised; she swung her legs and mimicked his open mouth.

"What about the boys?"

"You know they're dead to the world when there's a football game on. How about it, huh, mister?"

He cocked his head; then he went over and locked the door. When he came back she began to unbuckle his pants.

"What about your diaphragm?"

"I've been wearing it all day. In case something came up."

He couldn't help but grin. She slid her hands under the waist of his pants and down around the cheeks of his ass, then looked up at him.

"Honey, I'm sorry about downstairs."

"It's not as if I like spending my life working in the mill."

"I know. It's just that things weren't going so good for us for a while. And now that they are going good, it seems a shame we can't be together more."

"There's no reason why things can't keep getting better."

As she lay back and pulled him on top of her, he pushed her skirt up around her waist. Braced on one elbow, he worked her panties down far enough to free one leg, then entered her, his own pants down around his knees. Their rhythm was smooth and effortless, as always, well-practiced; as he watched her work her head methodically into the pillow, he thought This is good, this is really good, this is as good as it's ever going to get.

Four

He worked as a rolling mill maintenance supervisor, only it wasn't at the rolling mill in town; he worked at the mammoth S & W Tube Mill at Alum Rock—he tried working at Buchanan Steel in Furnass when he first got out of high school, when he and Myrna were first married, worked there for several years but found it was too close to home, found he couldn't stand the thought that his entire life was contained in this one little town, that anyplace he needed to go was within a one-mile radius of the house where he was born. Alum Rock was only ten minutes away, on the other side of the Ohio River, but at least it wasn't Furnass.

He was early for his shift, as he knew he would be, and drove past the mill entrance and the parking lots, down River Road several miles, and pulled into Fox's Motel. The woman at the desk recognized him but said nothing; she gave him the room he liked at the end of the building without asking. It was a small room paneled in cheap veneer to make it look like a cabin. There was barely enough room to walk between the straight chair and the cigarette-scarred end table, the tipsy floor lamp and the nightstand. On the wall above the bed was a large painting, a landscape of a covered bridge over rocky water, a boy in a straw hat fishing upstream. Vince turned on the lamp rather than the overhead so it would be cozy, made sure the heat was on before locking the door again, leaving the key under the mat. Driving back to the mill, there was snow in the air, a chill that would last for months now, the undeniable settling in of winter. The world was in negative as the snow started to stick, white hills, black trees; the only color in the late afternoon was the yellow-and-orange glow of the Bessemers at Furnass across the river, flickering against the lowered sky. Outside the gate of the mill, he stopped at a phone booth. Ernie the bartender recognized his voice and told him to hang on, he'd get her.

"Cindy, can you talk?"

"Only a minute. We're pretty busy. Why aren't all these people at home?"

"Are we still on for tonight?"

"I wasn't sure you'd still want to. With the holiday and all. Lot of family time."

"Of course I want to. I can make it all night if you can."

"How'd you manage that? No, don't tell me." She paused a moment; he could hear the bustle of the restaurant behind her. "You really want to see me, don't you?"

"Yeah, I really do."

"I can hear it in your voice. Spending time with your family must've made you realize how much you love me. I'll call my sister and have her keep the kids overnight."

"I'll be there as soon as I can after my shift. The key's under the mat if you get there first. Make it as soon as you can."

He hung up and stood there for a while, resting his weight against the cold glass. The wind worked little swirls of snow under the bottom of the walls around his feet. Beyond the guardhouse and the cyclone fence, the lights of the mill burned high overhead in the dusk, galaxies of work lights. He pushed, and the door folded to let him out; he walked, shoulders hunched with the cold, back to his pickup. No, she was wrong, he hadn't found out how much he loved her, or even if he loved her at all. But he did find out that he was going to do it anyway.

. . . The slope evens out beyond the bank of the creek bed. It is the top of a hill within the valley, a step of land above the river but much below the rim of the valley's hills. A table, a shelf, of ancient primeval forest. Beech and sugar maple, red oak and yellow birch, dating from the time when trees first grew here in this valley. The trunks are monstrous, six and eight feet in diameter, spaced well apart, the question of which would survive and which wouldn't decided centuries ago. A hundred feet overhead, however, the branches form a near solid vault of leaves. Here in autumn, the red and yellow leaves are luminous, resplendent in the afternoon light. But their light doesn't carry very far. It fades through the high still air, down the great trunks, down to the floor of the forest. The ground cover of moss and ferns glows darkly. It is a place of magic. Still as a catacomb, solemn as a shrine.

All his life Duncan has heard the stories. The stories of the other worlds, and those who can see them. He's heard the stories of the silkies, the seal people, who live in another world under the sea. The seals who come on land and take off their skins and become as people. The seals who father earthly children and then come back to claim them, take them with them to swim with the seals, back to their other world. He's heard the stories of the spirits of the woods, the glastigs, how they show themselves to some people to bring messages from other worlds. The story of his kinsman, a hunter, who heard a clacking in the woods one day. A sound like someone clacking stones together, or stags butting heads. The hunter followed the sound till he came to an old woman. She was crouched beside a rock, her head covered with a great green shawl, striking a pair of deer shanks together. She cried sorrowfully, "All my poor ones, all my poor ones." But when the hunter reached to console her and ask what she was talking about, the woman disappeared. When he returned home, he found that the MacDonalds of the Isles had been there and killed his wife and children.

All his life he had felt the presence of something else. Something around him, something with him. Unseen, beyond explanation. A presence, a force. Something. He wasn't particularly intelligent, others sometimes considered him to be a bit slow. He was ordinary, a peasant, of simple beliefs. He had heard the stories of those with the second sight, stories of fairies and spirits and other worlds, and wondered if they were part of what he feels. But he is no seer. The world he sees is only this world. The time he sees is only the present. He told the Campbell that he saw him covered in blood, carried like a sheep on the shoulders of the slaughterman, but it wasn't true. He only said it so the Campbell would leave him alone. The same as he let his mates go on thinking he has the second sight after Bushy Run. That way he doesn't have to tell them what he has seen. He lets them think he can see other worlds so he doesn't have to tell them what he has seen of this one.

Duncan walks on. His footsteps are cushioned by the moss and ferns. He listens for the crows by the river. And wonders if what he saw by the rocks was an Indian after all. Maybe it was a giant crow, the King of the Crows, come to tell him something. . . .

SALLY FURNACE

1960

One

Angelo wrestled a coil of wire rope. The older man got it up as high as his shoulder when it started to unwind, the coils slithering off one another, the end flopping around like a live thing. Finally he dumped the whole mess on the floor. "Son of a bitch!"

The young engineer from the front office was upset. "Come on, you guys, they're almost here. Help get that wire out of the way." He turned to Ted. Ted spread open his fireproof jacket, folded his hands under the bib of his fireproof overalls.

"I'm a weight-lifter," Ted leaned down toward the young man's ear. At the opposite end of the charging floor, One Furnace was coming to the end of its heat, but the roar—like a rocket going off, like a tornado in progress—still made talking difficult. "I wait while the other guys lift."

Ted straightened up again and grinned, proud of his little joke. It took the young man a moment to get it; when he did, he didn't like it. Ted pointed to the operating engineer's button on his hard hat and leaned forward again. "Different union. I touch that wire and we'll both be looking for new jobs. Got to learn how these things work, son."

The young engineer gave him a dirty look and hurried off to find someone else. The charging floor was elevated above the ground level of the BOF Shop like a mezzanine, like a stage, running the length of the long narrow building—a cavern of steel to make steel—in front of the furnaces. Below the metal railing, a cinder-pot railcar was moved out from under the floor where he was standing, the bowl of white-hot slag shimmering with the car's slightest movement. The heat hurt Ted's eyes, but he moved away slowly from the railing, he didn't want anyone to think that standing above the molten slag bothered him or anything like that. He took up a new position a few feet back from the railing.

"So what the hell are they doing?" Malachek said, coming over to him and leaning on his shovel. Because of the noise even casual conversation on the floor was conducted at the level of a shout. "Are they really going to name one of the oxy furnaces?"

Ted shrugged, made a face, rocked back on his heels.

"Nobody names an oxy furnace, do they?" Fast Eddie said. "I thought they only named blast furnaces."

"Son of a bitch, son of a bitch," Angelo said, still trying to get the coil of wire rope out of the way, kicking at it.

"Some bigwig thinks it's cute to have his daughter's name on a big piece of equipment," Malachek said. "I'll show her a big piece of equipment."

As long as he had an audience, Ted thought he'd take advantage of it. "Look at it this way. If they go to the trouble of naming the oxy furnaces, that's one more reason why they're not going to shut the plant down. Right?"

"All that talk about the mills closing," Angelo said, giving up on the wire rope, "that's bullshit. The mills aren't going nowhere. What's the country going to do if it can't make steel, huh? That's bullshit."

"Hey, here she comes!" Fast Eddie said, hitting Ted on the arm and scuttling down the railing away from the heat of the slag car. Ted looked at the spot on his arm where Fast Eddie hit him, looked after Fast Eddie, then followed him down the railing with the others.

Two

Coming through the gloom at the far end of the building was a group of a dozen men, all wearing white hardhats and white smocks over their suits. The men picked their way gingerly across the dirt floor, careful of their shoes, careful of the machinery and the debris and scrap metal lying around—the group ducked in unison as the hook of the traveling crane sailed through the building twenty feet above their heads, then looked around and laughed among themselves for being so scaredy—escorting, though actually most of them following, a girl.

She looked to be in her early twenties, no more than that certainly, a pretty girl though almost too slight, almost skeletal, the skirt of her pink suit too short either for the occasion or for her skinny legs. In her arms she cradled a bouquet of long-stemmed roses; the white hardhat on her head wobbled and threatened to slide off her long dark hair every time she moved. One man took her arm to help her over a set of tracks. The rest of the men tried to talk and joke with her to put her at ease, though most of the men seemed bothered more by the noise and confusion than she did. As the group got closer, below where Ted and Fast Eddie and a few others were watching, heading toward the elevator, the girl looked up, one hand placed firmly on top of her hardhat to hold it in place, and smiled. Then she was gone, all the white hats moving under the edge of the floor. She's a child, Ted thought, a goddamn kid.

"Did you see that, Ted?" Fast Eddie said as he went over to pick up his broom. "She looked right at me. Come to me, baby. Twelve-inch Eddie will take care of you."

"Hey Angelo," Nali, the foreman, said, coming over to them. "They're almost here, where's your necktie?"

"Son of a bitch," Angelo said. "She looks like a nice Italian girl."

"She looks like she'd like to suck on this," Malachek said. He clutched his rolled-up glove in front of his crotch. Angelo slapped it out of his hand and across the floor.

"What'd you do that for?" Malachek said. "I'll take you apart, old man."

Angelo looked like he wanted the other man to try it but Nali stepped between them. "Both of you together can't take me, so forget it. That would look great, wouldn't it? Board of directors comes here and you two are beating on each other."

"*Pazzo*," Angelo muttered. "*Stupido*."

Malachek went over and picked up his glove and drifted away as the elevator at the rear of the floor opened and the group of white hats stepped out.

They led the girl out of the shadows, along the passageway between the furnaces and out onto the front of the charging floor. A PR man exchanged the dozen roses she carried for a bottle of champagne and a photographer posed the girl and several of the men in white hardhats and smocks in front of the furnace. The basic oxygen furnace was a large pear-shaped steel cylinder mounted on trunnions in an open berth; the floor was cut away in front of it so the furnace could tilt forward and back. Because of the cutaway in the floor, the PR man realized the girl couldn't get close enough to the furnace to hit it with the bottle. The white hats held a hurry-up conference—the workmen standing around thought it was a pretty good joke—and someone came up with the idea of using the charging buggy for the dedication.

The PR guy talked to one of the white hats, who talked to another of the white hats, who directed another of the white hats to talk to Nali. Nali came over and told Ted to move the charging buggy to a position in front of the furnace. Ted shrugged, and as the other workmen hooted—then grew quiet again with a look from Nali—Ted walked down the track to where the charging buggy sat near Two Furnace. The charging buggy was twenty feet tall, a steel framework supporting a dump box loaded with tons of scrap metal. Ted operated it from a control panel that dangled down on a thick cable. As he trailed alongside the lumbering buggy, its siren trumpeting through the hollow building, Ted looked as if he walked it on a leash. When the men in the white hardhats saw that something that large could move—and was headed their direction—they stepped back and kept an eye on it as if afraid it might do something dreadful.

Three

After Ted positioned the buggy in front of the furnace, he reset his hardhat on the back of his head and sauntered over to where the PR man, a squared-off guy with a face like a pink boxing glove, was telling the girl how to hold the bottle for the photograph. He looked at Ted, obviously displeased at the interruption.

"You know, if she's going to break that bottle"—Ted leaned over to him—"she better put on some goggles."

"If she puts on goggles, they'll hide her face for the picture," the PR man said.

Ted interlaced his fingers under his bib; the man's nose was approximately at the level of Ted's chest. "That's better than getting a piece of glass in her eye. Isn't it?"

The PR man thought about that briefly. Then turned to the other men in white hardhats. "That's our safety-minded workmen for you, heh heh."

The men in white hardhats said, "Heh heh."

The young engineer quickly produced an extra pair of goggles, blushing as he handed them to the girl. She was still holding the bottle of champagne as she tried to slip the goggles over her hardhat; the strap became tangled in her hair. When nobody else made a move to help her, Ted went over and adjusted the band for her, fitting the goggles carefully over her eyes. It occurred to him that she was the same age as his girls; his daughters wanted little to do with him now but when they were small they'd run to meet him after work, liked to wear Daddy's goggles and try on his gloves: "Tell us about the mill, Daddy, tell us ple-e-e-ease." The girl looked up at him gratefully.

"It's a little hard to see," she said, twisting her head around, afraid to take a step.

"You get used to them," he grinned.

"Where should I hit it?"

Ted looked at the PR man but he only glared back; the white hats looked at each other. Ted took her by the elbow and escorted her over to the charging buggy, pointing out an area for her on the black-and-white-striped bumper. The photographer said that was great, great. The girl gripped the bottle by the neck and took a couple of practice swings.

"Just don't put a dent in my buggy with that thing, okay?" Ted said. The girl looked puzzled, then realized it was a joke and laughed too much.

On the signal from the photographer she took a windup and broke the champagne against the side of the buggy. She giggled and gave a little curtsy to everyone, the front of her pink suit soaked; the men in white hardhats applauded, a few of the workmen cheered. As the visitors stood back, the furnace tilted forward a few degrees and Ted worked the controls to raise the rear end of the charging buggy, dumping the tons of scrap metal into the concentric opening at the top of the furnace. Then he walked the buggy down the tracks out of the way. When he came back the white hardhats were busy talking among themselves; the girl was on the edge of the group talking to the photographer, but she watched Ted as if wondering what he was going to do next. Ted smiled at her and she left the others and came over to him. She looked at him as if he were her special friend.

"Is the furnace going now?" She leaned up to speak close to his ear, resting her hand on his arm for balance. There wasn't as much noise now that One Furnace had finished its heat but he was glad she did it anyway. He could smell her, clean like soap.

"Not really."

All the white hats were talking among themselves so Ted thought What the hell; he took her by the elbow again and guided her to a spot near the front of the furnace. He motioned to the operator inside the pulpit. Slowly the furnace tilted forward more so they could see inside. The men in white hardhats took a few steps back. The lining of the furnace glowed red, the pile of scrap metal at the bottom twinkled with the heat. The girl stood slightly behind him, squeezing his arm as she scrunched up against him to peer in the opening.

"It's two thousand degrees in there," he said to the side of her face, his lips almost touching her hair. "That hot enough for you?"

She laughed happily, looking up at his face, then leaned forward, gripping his arm for support, to look deeper inside. He put his other hand on her sleeve; he wouldn't have let anything hurt her for the world. The photographer came running over shouting, "Hold it, that's a great shot!" and got the two of them standing in front of the furnace.

Then a warning siren whooped repeatedly through the hollow building, shrieking like something wounded. Suspended from the overhead crane, the huge hot-metal ladle, shimmering with the heat of the molten metal inside, came gliding slowly toward them out of the darkness, specter-like and terrible.

"Watch this," he said as he leaned down to her again—the ends of her hair curling out from under the hardhat rested against his cheek, too soft to be prickly—and guided her back out of the way. "When the lance with the oxygen comes down and hits the hot metal, it'll light up in here like a cave of gold."

"Cave of gold?" she laughed, covering her mouth, as if delighted.

Ted nodded, full of knowledge.

The furnace rolled upright again to accept the molten pig iron, the berth exploding briefly with orangish-yellow light. As soon as the ladle was out of the way, the oxygen lance descended from the hood above the furnace, lowering into the bell of the cylinder. The pure oxygen hit the hot metal with a roar and a shower of sparks and flame that drove everyone back except the workmen, this end of the building full of blinding yellow-white light. He turned around to her to say, "See? A cave of gold!"—he wanted to tell her everything he knew about it, he wanted to tell her that in twenty-seven minutes they made as much steel in an oxy furnace as one of the old Bessemer converters made in an entire day, that they used enough oxygen during one heat to send a rocket to the moon and back—but in the noise and white-hot light, the group of men in white hats and smocks closed ranks around her and led her back toward the elevator. As the doors closed, the girl was laughing with the PR guy about something, Ted didn't know what, before they all descended out of sight. As the group of white hardhats headed back across the floor of the shop Ted stood at the railing away from the furnace, one foot up on the lower rail, ready to wave in case she looked back. But she didn't.

Some of the other workmen drifted over to where Ted stood at the railing. At the distant end of the building, the figures in the white coats and hats appeared less than an inch tall. They were gathered in a semicircle around one man who gestured here and there, pointing out things to the others. Then they disappeared one by one into the farther shadows. On the charging floor, the white-hot light danced and careened around the workmen, the heat beating against their backs as the furnace continued to blow. The men had to shout louder than ever to be heard.

"How's it feel to be a hero?" Nali said, putting his hand on Ted's shoulder. "A star?"

"She seemed like a nice girl, didn't she?" Fast Eddie said.

"See? I told you," Angelo said. "A nice Italian girl."

Malachek leaned on the railing, flicked his fingers under his chin at the departing figures. "After her with her." He looked at Ted.

Ted spread open his fireproof jacket, folded his hands under the bib of his fireproof overalls. "I'd fuck her," he said and turned away.

. . . *On the second day at Bushy Run, the Indians taunted them through the early morning haze: "Petticoat warriors, we will eat your eyes." And they held up the bodies of two Highlanders captured the day before. The men had been stripped and their genitals cut off, then roasted alive. Flesh was missing where the Indians had cut off chunks to eat in front of the dying men. The Indians laughed through the forest as they spread-eagled the bodies and made them dance. Other Indians carried the Highlanders' heads mounted on poles. When the Indians finally attacked in earnest, Duncan found it a relief.*

It was his first battle. He had fought before, in the Highlands, on cattle drives when they were attacked by robbers or rival clans. He had known fear before. He knew it as something to overcome within himself, something to beat down. A narrow ledge he had to cross simply because he was afraid of it so much—he couldn't rest otherwise. A part of him even liked it. He had known his own rage and fury before. He had known the fury of someone else trying to kill him. He had encountered savagery before, including his own. All that was familiar to him, all that he could understand. But he saw something else in the faces of the Indians as they held up the bodies of the tortured men. Heard something else in their laughter and taunts. Something that haunted him. Drew him to even greater rage within himself. By the time later that morning when his company was called upon to feign a retreat then turn around and charge, he seemed invincible. He flowed through what was happening around him, and what was happening flowed through him, in a terrible perfection. He ran between the trees, crashed out of the brush to find an Indian painted half-red half-black directly in front of him. The Indian took one look at him and fled. Duncan didn't take time to fire. He dropped the musket and ran after him, kilt hiked up around his groin, screaming the

MacKenzie battle cry, *"Tullochard!"* He brought down the fleeing
Indian with a swing of his broadsword, hamstrung him. The man
rolled on the ground clutching the back of his leg, tried frantically
to roll away from him. Duncan had time to see the man's eyes
before he drove the point of his broadsword two-handed through
the man's throat.

He ran to ground four more that morning. Hacking and slashing to bring them down, hacking and slashing all the more because
their backs were turned toward him, a rage he couldn't contain.
And then something within him seemed to give way. He was suddenly very very tired, he couldn't go a step farther. He sat down
and leaned back against a tree, his broadsword in his lap, and fell
asleep. He dreamt he was chasing another Indian through the
forest when the Indian suddenly stopped and turned around to
face him. The Indian was half-red half-black, but one side was
covered with blood and the other side was covered with black
feathers. As Duncan watched, the red side became covered with
black feathers too, and the man's head turned into that of a bird.
He was a crow, the King of the Crows, and a dozen crows sang
attendance in the trees. Duncan woke to find a dozen crows in
the trees around him, cawing. On the ground in front of him, a
large crow paraded back and forth, watching him. The bird
stopped, blinked, and opened its beak as if about to say something,
tell him something. Then something startled the birds and they
flew away. Duncan chased after them but he couldn't keep up.
Was the bird really going to tell him something? Were they some
kind of sign? When the other soldiers found him in the woods,
they thought Duncan had the second sight, but it was just the
opposite; the truth was he was looking for it, desperately. Something from some other world to explain to him this world. To help
him understand why he was filled with overwhelming loathing and
terror and disgust. Why he never wanted to fight, never wanted
to experience that savagery—his own savagery—again.

Holding On

And now this Campbell corporal in front of him seems determined to lead them into places of savagery and terror again. Black Duncan follows, but he searches the treetops. *Crow, crow, have you any songs for me?* . . .

MEETING OF MINDS

1986

For a second I flash on the idea that maybe I've fallen into a coal
shaft or something, that maybe I'm in a tunnel or a mine or
someplace deep underground, maybe even one of those mines
where they grow mushrooms. Because the place is pitch-dark, I
can't see a thing, but I don't need a light to tell me it's dirty
down there, I can feel it on me, all over me. Not just dusty, I
mean really dirty, the kind of dirt that sticks to you like grease
or something, grimy. I feel like I crawled through a lube rack
instead of through a transom window into her cellar—there's got
to be fifty years of soot from the mills all over everything down
there. And it stinks. I'm afraid maybe a sewer has backed up or
something and maybe there's shit all over the floor but I scuffle
my feet around a little and it seems dry enough. I figure that's
just the way the place smells, but it sure is awful.

> "I was sitting at the table in the dining room, go-
> ing over my Sunday school lesson for the next day,
> and brushing my hair. I guess it must have been
> pretty late, maybe one thirty or two in the morning,
> something like that, I'm usually up that late now. I
> don't sleep that much anymore, at least not at night,

though during the day I'll usually lie down and take
a nap on the couch. Me and the cat."

So I stand there in the dark a couple minutes, trying to get
my head to stop spinning. I still can't see my hand in front of my
face, and I'm all dirty, and I must've pulled a muscle in my leg
climbing up over that door. And maybe I've had too much foolish
powder or something, I don't know, but all of a sudden I start
laughing to myself, you know, giggling. I can't stop. It seems like
the funniest thing in the world, me standing there in the old
dolly's basement, especially after she's gone to so much trouble
to try to keep people out. I mean, she's put new locks on the
doors and boarded up the cellar windows—that's why it's so dark
down there, there's only little cracks of light from the streetlight
outside—but she forgot about the transom over the basement
door. Either that or she didn't forget about it at all, she figured
the only person that could ever squeeze through a little opening
like that is somebody small and wiry like me, and I just have to
stand there until I stop giggling because, I don't know, it seems
so funny.

"And I was watching television too, I think it was
a rerun of *Ironsides*, that's about all I watch nowadays, that and the news and maybe a football game
if the Steelers play. I know it must have been fairly
late because I was finally getting dozy. I'd drop off
for a little bit and then the cat would get up on the
table and say something and wake me up again. Then
I'd read a little more of the lesson—Daniel 3, about
King Nebuchadnezzar and his graven image, and the
way the angel of the Lord delivered Shadrach, Meshach, and Abednego from the fiery furnace. It's one
of my favorite stories, I always remember the way

Dickie—my youngest when he was a little boy—used to call them Shadrach, Meshach, and Into-Bed-I-Go. And then brush my hair and watch television a little more before I'd doze off again."

I can hear the television blasting away upstairs, coming through the floorboards over my head, and I know the old dolly is home. The house has these great big windows and she doesn't close the drapes most of the time so you can look right in and see what she's doing. It's a big old house at the end of Fifth Avenue, the last house on the street, back there all by itself—the street isn't even paved, it's only oiled and all broken up—sitting among the trees like a mansion or something, on the edge of the bluffs of Orchard Hill overlooking the rest of Furnass. Sometimes I wonder if she leaves the drapes open like that on purpose, so you *can* see what she's doing. So I can see what she's doing. Because that's sort of why I'm there. I mean, I always see her at Mikey's All-Niter, where me and the other guys hang out in the evenings. She's a good-looking dolly for being older and all—I don't know, she's sixty or seventy or something, that's why we call her the old dolly—but for an old dolly she's got a great pair of legs. All the guys think so. She wears these high heels all the time, and outfits that show off her legs, and I mean—they're a great pair of legs. And lately whenever she comes into Mikey's All-Niter, getting in or out of her car or something, she always seems to look at me, I mean not exactly flirty or anything, but you know, looks at me, watches me watching her, like she knows I'm watching her and watching her legs and she's not mad or upset about it or anything. Like she, well—I don't know. Like she leaves the drapes open like that so I can come and watch her, like she is inviting me or something. I break into other houses on the Hill all the time but those houses belong to old old women, most of the time they're sitting there in their chairs half-asleep and I can walk right by them and they never even see me. But I've never been in the old dolly's house before, and I'm not sure why I'm there now, and I'm beginning to wonder if I know what I'm getting myself into.

"I knew that someone had been in the house before. I knew there was a man out there in the woods. Nobody ever took me seriously about it, I guess they think I'm just getting old, that I'm getting to be a funny old woman, but I knew a man had been in the house and taken some things. Nothing big, mind you, only little things, ten dollars here, twenty dollars there, or sometimes he'd only move things around so they wouldn't be in the same place where I left them. I tried to tell people about the man but they only humored me. When I told the police about him they only smiled and told me to get some more locks for the doors, they wouldn't even take a look. Dickie finally came over and helped me board up the windows in the basement but he only did it because I'm his mother. I kept a lookout whenever I went to the store to see if I could single out anybody who looked like the type to do such a thing, but most of the time at Mikey's All-Niter there were only boys being boys, loafing around when they should be home doing their homework. I suppose everybody thought I was just a funny old woman living alone who kept losing things. But I knew there was a man out there, out there among the trees at the end of the yard watching the house, and I kept all the drapes pulled back so he would know I was here, and maybe I could get a good look at him and identify him to the police. I was sure that sooner or later he'd try to get inside."

My eyes are gradually getting used to the dark, but I still can't see very well, there isn't enough light. About all I can make out is that the room I'm in is piled high with stuff, in some places almost to the ceiling, I seem to be standing in the only clear spot in the entire room. There's stacks of boxes and pieces of old furniture and a broken stepladder and a lawn mower and piles of moldy books—anything you can think of. And then I look up, and all around the room are these old bicycles and tricycles and kiddie cars tied up to the ceiling with clothesline, like they've floated up to the top of the room or something. And then a car must have turned around at the end of the street because a little beam of light sweeps over them and makes the bikes and trikes and kiddie cars look like they're gliding past, ghost riders in the sky. It's like a dream down there.

"And I guess I am getting older and maybe I am turning into a funny old woman, at least to them. I sleep when I want to and I eat when I feel like it and I talk to the cat all the time, and I keep this big old house filled with things that most people consider junk. Maybe I am getting old, maybe I am getting peculiar. But I'll tell you, this is the first time in my entire life that I can do things when and if and how I want to, not when somebody else wants them or when somebody else lets me. And the cat is certainly more company and more affectionate than any of my children turned out to be—oh sharper than a serpent's tooth. And as for the house, all these things I've saved and keep here are tangible proof to me that my life actually happened, that I didn't imagine it or dream it, my life's been very good to me. And those memories are certainly better and more

satisfying and mean more to me than any of your so-
called reality I've seen lately. So if that qualifies me
to be called a funny old woman, then you can count
me in."

And then this really weird thing happens. I don't know, maybe
my head is still messed up. Or maybe I'm feeling guilty or something about being down there where I know I'm not supposed to
be, or maybe I'm thinking about whatever it was I thinking when
I had the idea to break into the house in the first place. Or maybe
I start picking up on some kind of bad vibration from the place.
Whatever it is, I start to get spooked. I mean, here I am, I'm the
one breaking into the house, right? And I'm the one getting
scared. Because I swear there's something going on down there,
something evil. And I don't like not being able to see very well,
and I don't like all this junk around me boxing me in, and I don't
like feeling all dirty and messy. It's almost like I'm starting to
feel something crawling all over me. And then I get this feeling
that something's watching me, something or somebody. So I'm
straining my eyes and looking all around and there they are, I see
these gold-green eyes looking down at me from on top of this pile
of stuff, not animal eyes but glassy staring dead eyes. And then
all of a sudden there's this great *Whoosh!* and a tongue of fire
leaps out across the floor and around my feet and I scream and
jump straight up in the air and bash my head into one of the
bicycles hanging from the ceiling.

"I hear things at night sometimes, it's true. I always have since I've lived here alone. Voices,
sounds—I suppose people would say that's another
sign that I've turned into a funny old woman. I know
this is a large house, too large for one woman, an old
woman alone. An old woman. The house settles and

the stairs creak and the radiators pop. But I don't mind, that's the point: I've always liked the noises, they're a comfort to me. They make me feel as though there actually is someone else in the house. I don't mean someone trying to break in, I mean as though the family were still here, as though Harry were still alive or the children were still children and living here at home and moving about in another part of the house. The noises make me feel as if I'm not really alone. Because they make it sound the way it was when somebody else actually was here."

The eyes turn out to belong to a large antique doll, and the tongue of fire is the light from the burners of the water heater beside me. But knowing all that doesn't seem to help much. The doll is really weird. It doesn't have any clothes on and its body is made out of cloth instead of skin and its arms and legs are all twisted around into positions that arms and legs should never be twisted into. And then I start thinking about what happens if the flames from the water heater leap out of there and set some of this stuff on fire, I'll be fried before I know it. So I forget about why I thought of seeing the old dolly or whatever I thought I was going to do here in the house, I want to get out of here as fast as I can but I don't know how. There seem to be paths through the maze of stuff but they don't go anywhere when I start to follow them—one dead-ends at an electrical box and another is a blind alley to the remains of a washing machine. Where I'm standing there's boxes piled up taller than my head, I can't even see the door I climbed over to get in here, and I start thinking I'm never going to get out of here, I'm going to die down here and nobody's ever going to know what happened to me, they'll find my body after the old dolly kicks off and they clear all this stuff out for a yard sale. I'm standing here with tears running down my

cheeks—even my tears taste like dirt—and I swear I'll never drink
or smoke or snort or shoot up again. At least before I go house-
breaking again.

> "But I don't think about loneliness much, I simply
> won't let myself. You see, I decided a while ago that
> I'm going to enjoy the rest of my life. I mean I know
> there's not much of it left, even though I'm not that
> old, and why should I waste what time there is by
> sitting around feeling sorry for myself? I decided I'm
> going to have a good time for myself, and if other
> people don't like it, or if I turn into a funny old
> woman, or if other people already think I am, well,
> that's their problem. After all, it's my life, I'm the
> one who's going to die, not somebody else."

Finally I get hold of myself and try to find my way back to
the door. But there's all these little stacks of magazines all over
the floor and when I step on them they start sliding around. I'm
slipping all over the place and the first thing I know I'm down on
the floor and scared to death something's going to fall on me and
bury me so they never will find me, ever. So I reach up for something to hold on to but I grab hold of a laundry basket and these
old drapes or curtains or something tumble all over me and the
more I try to get up the more they wrap themselves around me
like they're some kind of boa constrictors trying to suffocate me.
And I'm fighting and punching and kicking and finally I get myself free and stand up but I step on a pipe or bottle or something
that goes rolling out from under me and I'm back on the floor
again, only now I'm crawling through a pile of empty cardboard
boxes that she must've thrown down the cellar steps. But at least
I've found the cellar steps and I figure I'll get out that way, but
the steps are filled with mason jars and empty Pepsi bottles and

cans of cat food and large green plastic garbage bags filled with I don't know what, and I'm like a salmon trying to fight its way upstream, and one of the cardboard boxes is still attached to my leg like a pair of cardboard jaws and I think Holy shit I'm going to be eaten alive by a cellar full of junk.

> "And this house is part of me, I'd rather give up living than give up this house. If I did give up this house, I might as well give up living, because there wouldn't be anything to live for, now. This house is part of me, and I'm part of this house. I guess that's why I got so mad whenever I thought about that man trying to break into it."

There's a crack of light along the bottom of the door as I crawl up the last couple of steps, and I figure the way everything else is going the door is probably locked. But it isn't and I push it open a couple inches and come face-to-face with her big brown cat. I jump back and my hand slams into an ironing board that's hanging on the back of the door and the spring holding it gives way and the board starts to topple over and I try to grab it and I almost ride it like a surfboard back down the stairs before I get it stopped. It takes me a couple minutes but I finally get the board back into its holder so it'll stand upright again, and I have to wait a couple more minutes until my breath comes back. The whole time the cat is sitting there in the partially open doorway looking at me, bored. When it sees that nothing else interesting is going to happen, it turns around and walks into the dining room. I open the door a little further and peek around the corner to see if the coast is clear and it is, the old dolly is there all right, sitting at the table, but she's sound asleep, her head bobbing up and down against her chest like a cork on the river while the television set is blaring away in her ear. Real careful, I open the door wide enough for me to squeeze through and I tiptoe across the kitchen and I almost make it too, I almost make it to the back door when I conk my head on a cowbell that's hanging down from out of nowhere.

"So I was very proud of myself to come up with the idea of those cowbells. I know I don't always hear the doorbell anymore, and sometimes I forget to lock the back door or I don't close it all the way after the cat goes out—well, that man could have simply waltzed right in. And then I remembered I had this box of cowbells upstairs in the closet. I've always collected bells—you know those fancy elephant bells and sleigh bells and camel bells and all, the Bells of Sarna I think they're called. I have strings of them hanging in the doorways in the front rooms and I always think they look so nice. But I never knew what to do with all those old cowbells from my uncle's farm until I had an idea—oh there's so much the world has to offer if you'll only make use of it. Anyway, so I rigged five or six of the largest cowbells on a clothesline and hung them across the kitchen attached to the back door so they'd ring if anyone tried to come in, if that man tried to come in. Aren't I the clever one though?"

There's blood running down my forehead and into my eyes, and I can't tell for sure if it's my head or the cowbell that's still ringing. I look up and I can't believe it, there's cowbells strung all across the kitchen at just the right height to bonk anybody who's not paying attention. She's got the place booby-trapped. It's like she's been expecting me all right, like I thought, like she's been waiting for me, except that she's been waiting to get me.

The bell that clobbered me is still dancing around my head and clanking away so I reach up and grab it but that pulls the string and the bell next to it starts ringing too and then I try to grab it too and now the whole string of bells is bobbing up and down and clanking away and I look across the kitchen and there's the old dolly herself standing in the doorway watching me go crazy.

"I heard the bells ringing, I'm sure that's what woke me up, so I went out to the kitchen and sure enough, there he was, that man. I could tell right away that he was a hippie because he was so dirty, he looked like somebody had rolled him on a large ink pad, he was filthy. Those people certainly don't take care of themselves. And I knew he was high on something because he was standing there in the middle of the room playing with the cowbells. He'd ring one and then another and then another as if he thought he was a Swiss bell ringer, yodel-lay-ee-oooo!"

She looks like a scarecrow. I mean she doesn't look at all attractive to me, not the way she seemed when I'd see her at Mikey's All-Niter or when I'd look in her windows. Her hair's down around her shoulders like she's wearing a gray hood or something, and her face is all puffy with sleep—she looks exactly like what she is: somebody's mom—and she's wearing some kind of long peasant dress and instead of high heels she's got on sandals and her toes are all waving at me and I can't tell at this point whether she's got great legs or not and I don't care. I flash on the idea that she's the evil queen in "Snow White and the Seven Dwarfs" and that I've climbed out of the diamond mine or wherever it was the dwarfs worked and if I look through the house I'll find a beautiful young girl in a glass coffin sound asleep. That makes me giggle a little, but she's still standing there looking at me. I suppose she's groggy from being asleep, and there's no question about it, she's caught me red-handed, I'm standing there in her kitchen in the middle of the night. And she doesn't know why I've broken in there; she doesn't know if I'm there to kill her or rob her or rape her or what. So what do you think she does? Scream and yell for help? Run away? Grab a knife or something and try to defend herself? Nope. She waves her finger at me and starts to give me a good bawling out. Exactly like somebody's mom.

> "So I just told him, he had no business being there in my house, no business at all, and that I was sick and tired of fooling around with him and that if he didn't stop pestering me I was going to call the police. The very idea, breaking into my house like that. And looking that way too."

She's looking at me sort of funny, and I look down at myself and I'm covered with soot like I fell out of a chimney or something, there's little bits of dirt falling off me like black snow every time I move and my footprints have followed me all the way across the floor. And I can't help it, I start giggling again, but that gets her all the more wound up and she's talking like I'm a maniac or something so I figure what the hell, I might as well give the old dolly a show. So I go into a crouch sort of like those pictures downstreet in the window of the kung fu studio and start waving my fingers at her like the karate guys do.

> "Well, he started doing one of those modern disco dances I've seen on *American Bandstand*, and he looked at me as if he wanted me to do it with him. So I knew right then and there he was flipped out on

something as they say and that he might be dangerous. He should have known I was too old to do a
dance like that, even though I was a pretty fair
dancer in my day if I do say so myself. But I thought
I better humor him as much as I could, so I waved
my arms back at him and wagged my shoulders and
wiggled my hips a little while I backed slowly into
the dining room, and he started to come after me."

Every time I take a step forward, she takes a step backward,
it's like we're doing a tango or something. She's waggling her
arms around like she thinks she's one of those old-time hootchy-
kootchy dancers, and we're moving that way, step by step, out
of the kitchen and through a little entryway into the dining room.
For a few moments it's almost like I'm chasing her in slow motion, and then it occurs to me that maybe I'm not chasing her at
all, maybe she's drawing me in, maybe she's pulling me in after
her, and the reason why she's waving her arms around like that
is to put some kind of hex on me, like it's a voodoo ritual or
something. So I stop and straighten up and look around at where
I am—and all my circuits go on overload. Because I've never been
in a place like this before in my life: here it is the middle of the
night, it's pitch dark outside, and it's brighter in her dining room
than in anyplace I've ever seen. Every light in the room is on and
there's a lot of them. It's not like I'm standing in a spotlight
because the light is everywhere, there's floor lamps and table
lamps and wall lamps and a chandelier hanging down over the
table like an enormous sparkling egg. But it's not only the light
that gets to me. I'm standing in the middle of the knickknack
capital of the universe, there's more things in this one room than
in any other ten rooms I've ever seen, and all this stuff is looking
at me. There's dozens and dozens, maybe hundreds of little figu-
rines, little dogs and little cats and little boys fishing in mirrors

and plaster goldfish and little old men sitting in little old rocking
chairs; there's a pink cow standing on its own udder and there's
a purple cow doing nothing except being purple and there's a
crouching tiger stalking a mug in the shape of a man's head and
a little dismembered hand holding some green pills and a knobby
giraffe with its neck all twisted around so it can see between its
own legs. And the whole time the television is blaring away and
the big brown tabby cat is sitting on the edge of the table with a
silly expression on its face like it's laughing at me, like it's saying
She's really got you now, buster. I'm vaguely aware that while
I'm gawking around she's digging in a chest of drawers but all
that registers to me is that the drawer she opened looks like it's
filled with forty-eight dozen pairs of right-handed white gloves.

> "When he got into the dining room, he stopped
> and looked around. My guess is that he came from a
> poor family and he wasn't used to being in a really
> nice home, and now that he was here he wanted to
> take it all in. It's too bad the government or the DAR
> or somebody doesn't have a program like that, to
> take the poor and underprivileged on tours into the
> better homes so those people would be able to see
> nice things and know what it is they are all striving
> for. But I'm glad he did stop a moment to look
> around and appreciate everything, because it gave
> me time to open the chest of drawers and find my
> tranquilizer gun."

The first thing I know she's fiddling around with this metal
canister, she's poking it and pushing it in different places and I
recognize it as one of those cans of Mace you can buy at the
drugstore. Only she can't quite figure out yet how to make it
work and she's jiggling it and shaking it and turning it upside

down and I figure if she's not careful the damn thing is going to explode and really hurt somebody. But before I can do anything she sets it off in some way or other and this sort of slow cloud fizzles out of it in the general direction of the ceiling and neither me or the cat is going to wait around until she figures out how to aim it too. The cat and I have a footrace to get to the back door except that the cat is one hell of a lot shorter than I am and I bonk my head a couple more times on those cowbells and now I can hardly see straight much less hear anything but I know the old dolly is coming right behind me poking and jiggling her little can and finally I get the back door open and me and the cat squeeze by each other out into the night.

"I had a little trouble with the gun at first, I couldn't find the trigger or remember exactly how it worked. But I finally got it going and I'm sure I hit him, I'm pretty sure I squirted him a couple times with it. I chased him through the kitchen and on out the back door—that dreadful man, he let the cat out too—he ran across the yard and then jumped into the bushes and slid down the hillside and got away. I was very disappointed with the gun, I thought it was supposed to knock him out right there on the spot and I expected him to fall down and go right to sleep. But he was still moving the last time I saw him, darn it. You can't depend on anything you buy over at the drugstore anymore, not since that young couple took it over."

The cat heads for the trees and I head for the bushes except that the bushes are right on the edge of the bluff and the first thing I know I'm slipping and sliding and tumbling and falling down the hillside, grabbing on to dead branches and tree trunks and anything else I can to try to stop me and I think I'm going to tumble all the way down Orchard Hill and end up rolling like a pill bug down the main street of town. I finally get myself stopped and I lie there a while, enjoying just lying there. Then it takes me a while to climb back up the hill again and by that time I'm not only covered with soot from the old dolly's basement, I'm covered with twigs and burrs and dead leaves too. About the time I get myself back up to the top of the bluff the police car is bouncing slowly down the broken street and I hide in the bushes and watch as Officer Boyd and another cop climb out of the car and go inside the house. They're in there a while, I can see them moving around through the big windows, and then they're out in the yard poking around with their flashlights and making notes on their clipboards, the old dolly following along behind talking to them the whole time, pointing this way and that and sometimes right at where I'm hiding. Except in the time I was playing tumbleweed down the hillside and mountain goat to get back up, she's fixed herself up again. She's straightened her hair and she's put on another dress and she's wearing those high heels again that make her legs look so great and I can see Officer Boyd and the other cop appreciating her legs and her old dolly's ass every time she turns away. Then they go back in the house again and talk to her some more and look at her legs some more, I can see them as they go on into the kitchen. She tells them all about what happened and Officer Boyd and the other cop nod and make some more notes but I know they don't care about a thing like this, they'd only worry if I killed her or raped her or something. But I'm glad I stick around to watch. Because after Officer Boyd listens for a while and pats her on the shoulder and gets a good eyeful of her legs as she starts to leave the kitchen, he turns around and bonks his head on one of the cowbells.

"I called the police and this time they had to admit the man had actually been here, all right, there were footprints all over the place and I'm sure there were fingerprints too, but they still didn't do anything. I even told them I hit him with the tranquilizer gun and that all they had to do was climb down the hillside and I was sure they'd find him curled up sound asleep. But they only smiled and wrote something on their little pads and told me to put some more locks on the doors. To them I guess I'm only a funny old woman. They even started playing around with the cowbells themselves, grown men. But I know that man is still out there keeping an eye on the house, waiting for another chance to get back in here, waiting for a chance to get me. I have to keep watch for him all the time."

I finally give up and go home. It's been a while since I broke in there, and when I'm hanging out at Mikey's All-Niter and the old dolly comes in, I'm careful to stay out of sight. Somebody put another sheet of plywood over that transom, so it's better to lay low for a while and let things cool down. But I still keep an eye on the place. I lie in the bushes at night and watch the old dolly through her open drapes as she wanders from room to room, as she goes from window to window and stares out into the darkness as if she's waiting for something or somebody. As if she's waiting for me. And I know I can find a way in there when I want to, when the time is right. And I know she knows it too. Only the next time I'll be ready for that old dolly. Next time she won't think it's so funny.

. . . There's wind in the branches high overhead. The tall canopy of red and yellow and orange leaves, glowing with sunlight while still blocking out the sun, shifts and waves. In the patches where the leaves have already fallen, shafts of sunlight reach down through the gloom among the massive tree trunks, prod around on the floor of the forest, then disappear again. There is the continual distant rush of the leaves blowing a hundred feet above their heads; but the forest is quiet around them, there is only the occasional crunch of their footsteps in the leaves already on the ground. Drifting down, a few leaves are always falling, always falling, torn from the branches overhead but floating now in the high still air of the forest, seemingly forever. A bit of sunlight finds the brass plate on the front of Hugh Campbell's mitred bearskin hat. For a while the reflection precedes him through the forest, a bright coin of light rolling across the ground always out of reach, then blinks and fades and goes away completely.

He was used to the thin pretty trees of the mountains of Argyll. Not these great hulking monstrosities. In the Highlands there were tall slender cedars and pines. And the tree he thought of most when he thought of home, the weeping birch. Its delicate branches drooped almost to the ground around its thin white trunk like a girl's hair hanging long. The wind swept through the tiers of branches and set them swaying like a woman's skirt whirling in a reel. The forests of home were very different from this world where he finds himself now. As he walks along the forest spokes out from him on every side, but it's not the trees so much that disturb him, the bare trunks soaring above him like the columns of Saint Mungo's in Glasgow. It's the spaces that wheel between the trees that worry him, an endless series of paths leading in any number of directions. Or leading any number of Indians right to them. He wonders if he'll ever see the forests of home again.

He was with the Black Watch at Fort Ticonderoga in 1758, his first battle, when the men around him couldn't stand the slaughter any longer. They had stood in reserve all day, they had watched six or seven assaults fail, and they finally went against their orders and rushed forward to help the others. For four hours they hurled themselves against the abatis of fallen trees, hacking with their broadswords at the entanglement of sharpened branches through volleys of musket fire, stood on each other's shoulders and tried to claw their way up the earthworks. It took three direct orders to get them to retreat, and then they would only walk back to their lines, not run, still screaming their clan battle cries; they lost two-thirds of their officers that day, and half their men. He was at Ticonderoga again the following year when it fell, and at the brief siege of Montreal in '60. He was at the invasion of Martinique in '62, and the forty-day siege of Morro Castle and Havana, where disease did more to destroy their ranks than the fighting. He was at Bushy Run.

A bug is trying to work its way inside his collar. Hugh digs it out and looks at it—an earwig—snaps its back with his thumbnail and throws it away. He doesn't know what happened to this Mac-Murchie boy behind him that day at Bushy Run. He knows he can't expect any help from him now, the Black Lad's mind is away with the fairies and ghosts. He knows that he himself is not much better, he's bone-weary. But he swears to himself that he's going to get them both out of this alive. He swears that no one is going to hurt this sorry lad with him. They'll have to fight their way past a Campbell first. He listens. Somewhere far off in the woods there's a clacking, like someone beating two rocks together. . . .

A WHIFF OF SANCTITY

1978

When Frank told him the deal was final and Peregrini Brothers Men's Wear (Style to Suit!) was definitely going to sell their store—while the selling was good, according to brother Frank—to make way for a big new building project in town that wanted their location, it was left to brother Joe to tell the bad news to the Peregrinis' longtime tenants next door in the building, the Little People Shop. After all, that was the way the Peregrini brothers had always worked their business: Frank was Mr. Inside, he took care of the finances and paperwork; and Joe was Mr. Outside, he was the salesman and the one who was good with people. It only stood to reason that Joe would be the one to tell Whitey and Midge that, come the first of the month, the building was sold and going to be demolished and that they and their shop were out on their ears.

But this particular morning Joe wasn't thinking about the store or the fact that soon he wasn't going to have one—or what exactly he told Whitey last night when he took him out for a drink to tell him the bad news. Instead, Joe sat on a stool at the Furnass Grill imagining that a six-and-one-half-inch Capuchin monk hovered on the shelf behind the counter, on top of a stack of sundae glasses. The little monk spread his arms, trying to assume the standard Come-Unto-Me pose, but the glasses kept tinkling and his sandals couldn't get traction and tiny drops of blood from his stigmata dripped down the sides of the ribbed glassware.

"I guess it's hard sometimes to keep your balance around here, eh Giuseppe?" Joe envisioned the monk saying to him.

"Careful, Padre, that whole display is liable to come tumbling down."

"You say something, Joe?" Jo the waitress said.

"More coffee," Joe said. "And could you stop those glasses from making so much noise?"

"You got the whips and jingles again today, huh? Yeah, little noises like that can drive you crazy."

She settled the glasses so they didn't rattle with the vibrations from the exhaust fan; Joe pretended that she brushed the little priest away with her hand. The tiny Capuchin disappeared in a blue cloud somewhere near the milk-shake machine.

"Gone in a puff of smoke," Joe ruminated out loud.

"That's the way it goes, hon," Jo said.

He gave her his best salesman's smile and watched her walk down along the counter with the coffeepot. Her pillowy buttocks churning away within her waitress uniform looked to him like paradise.

After Joe came back from serving in World War II, after he had seen the real-life padre with the bleeding hands and feet in Italy, he had waited years for a sign, a vision of the miraculous priest that would answer all his questions once and for all. That would tell him that he, Joe Peregrini, was special and that God loved him; that would tell him, by the act of appearing to him at all, that there was in fact a God. But the sign never came, and gradually Joe gave up. Early this morning, however, as he lay in the gray light of dawn, awake as usual with only a few hours' sleep after he'd been drinking, something brought the idea to mind again; he imagined what it would be like to have a vision: a small glow on the other side of the bedroom, appearing over Ruth's dresser, becoming brighter and fuller as the image of the plump bearded monk grew to life-sized and floated down to the foot of the bed, the room suddenly full of the smell of flowers.

"Good morning, Giuseppe, I hope I didn't wake you."

"No, Padre, that's okay. What took you so long?"

"I'm sorry, my son, but there was turbulence over the Atlantic, and all the visions were stacked up over New York. . . ."

They said the padre often made his presence known with the smell of flowers—lilies or geraniums or roses—or with a smell much like that of cigarettes or incense, to show the faithful that their prayers were heard. But as Joe flapped the covers he realized the smell was definitely that of cigarettes and that it came only from himself: stale bar smoke, the smoke from Whitey's cigarettes. He hacked lightly; his breath was putrid. He and Whitey must have closed the Riverside Inn, but he couldn't remember for sure; any more than he could remember driving home or climbing in beside Ruth. Nor could he remember if he told Whitey as he intended to about the sale of the building, told him that his and Midge's cute little children's shop was soon to be a heap of rubble. He guessed he did, he hoped he did—he wondered how Whitey took it. He looked over at the lump of his wife. Ruth rolled over and adjusted the covers about her; she smelled of sleep and woman and tomato sauce. At least he knew what he missed for dinner.

Slowly, and oh so carefully, he got up—his stomach felt like a chunk of ice; the dim room kept sliding down the walls, jumping up and sliding down again—dressed, bumped down the hall to the bathroom, pissed, washed, doused himself with Brut, and left the house. The sun barely cleared the rim of the valley's hills across the river; the angled light threw strong shadows along the block and set the paving bricks in bold relief, a street of measured cracks. The leaves of the sycamores and maples, already changed with the season, caught the autumn sunlight and glowed yellow and red as if lit from within. As he started to back the car out of the driveway, he thought he saw Ruth, her puffy sad-eyed face, her hair in curlers, watching from their bedroom window. He heard the scream just in time and braked. Behind him, a couple of grade school kids gave him the finger after he almost ran them over. If Ruth had been watching from the upstairs window, she was gone now. Joe rested his head on the steering wheel.

"That's all I'd need in this town," he said to himself. "Run over a couple kids in my own driveway while still drunk from the night before. What would the good padre think of that?"

"I would not like it, Giuseppe. That's not what the Lord meant when He said, 'Suffer the little children.'"

On the dashboard was a white plastic statue of the Sacred Heart. Joe pretended it was a small Italian monk, the little plastic hands and feet bright red with little painted stigmata; as Joe watched the little figure did a buck-and-wing, ending with a bow and a tip of his halo. Joe drove on down the hill a few blocks to Holy Innocents.

Inside the church, the Angelus rang down from the tower; the bells sounded hollow and wavy, but Joe thought maybe he wasn't hearing right. Children filled most of the pews, except for the last two rows that were taken up mainly by old women fingering rosaries. As old Monsignor Ifft came into the sanctuary and the boys' choir launched into the Kyrie, Joe eased himself down onto a padded kneeler behind the last pew. He didn't like the ceremony much anymore; since they ecumenicalized it there didn't seem to be much to it, he could understand every word. But he didn't like to think that the only reason he started coming to daily mass again was Janet Fabrizio. She knelt in the row in front of him, a heavyset attractive girl in her mid-twenties; this morning she was wearing a red-and-white-striped dress and a black lace mantilla over her head. Rumor had it that Janet Fabrizio went to mass every morning, before going to work at Sutcliff Realty, to make up for the fact that she gave blow jobs to a number of local businessmen at night. Joe had no proof of that, of course; if it was true, he wasn't a member of the select—the story of his life. But Janet Fabrizio seemed to give him a special smile every time he saw her at church, and he wanted to see if he could keep his string going.

The church was stuffy and he felt woozy from the smells of incense and flowers and perfume. He leaned his head against the marble pillar beside him as if it were an old friend; the stone was cool on the side of his forehead, a comfort. There was the smell of cigarettes too, but he decided that it must come from himself, it must be on his skin, in his hair. The smell of perfume he guessed came from Janet Fabrizio—could the holy padre come on the wings of Charlie or Chanel? He smiled to himself and gazed around the church. On the sidewall was the altar to Our Lady of Fatima, a rack with a hundred votive candles flickering in front of it. If these little old ladies thought they were devoted now, Joe could imagine the wailing and beating of withered breasts if they saw the holy monk trying to squeeze into the niche beside the plaster Virgin.

"Giuseppe, excuse me for interrupting the mass and all, but I wanted to speak to you."

"Padre, you're scaring these people half to death."

"I know, I know, forgive me. Everything here in America is very confusing." The monk tried to shoulder a little more room for himself beside the statue, but the Virgin got fed up with him and gave him a little kick, knocking him off his cloud.

Joe giggled, which he pretended was a cough when some of the old women turned around to look at him; he had to get ahold of himself. He came back to his senses as Janet Fabrizio stood up and worked her way across the pew to go to communion. In the aisle, she tottered briefly on her high heels, then walked to the front of the church, her lips kissing her prayerful fingertips, her full candy-striped skirt flouncing with every step. In a few moments she returned, her mouth set as she held the Host on her tongue. As she sidestepped back to her place in the pew, she looked at Joe and smiled and swallowed hard.

Lord! Joe said to himself. He genuflected quickly, blessed himself with holy water from the font, and leaned against the heavy studded door with every bit of strength he could muster to push his way back outside. He was halfway down the front steps when Father Mulroy appeared from the rectory and called to him. The young priest came gliding toward him, his black cassock sweeping over the sidewalk as if he were mounted on casters.

"Good morning, Joseph. I was hoping I'd see you here sometime this week."

"What's up, Father? Want to come down to the store and change an old habit, ha ha?"

As Joe should have known by now, the ascetic Father Mulroy had no sense of humor. "I'm still waiting to see those pictures of your stigmatic priest."

His stigmatic priest. Well, maybe he was too. Joe had been wounded at Monte Cassino and spent time in an Italian hospital; near the village where he was recuperating was a monastery with a monk who was said to bleed continuously from his hands and feet in imitation of the wounds of Christ. When Joe eventually returned home he had no particularly good war stories to tell— he was shot in the leg his second day at the front and he himself was the only person he had ever seen wounded—so instead he told everybody about the miraculous priest. The stories turned out to have a ready-made audience. The old-country people in the parish and around town welcomed any word of Italy, and they ate up everything Joe told them about the padre with the same fervor and devotion he had witnessed there. He told them about the miracles the monk was said to perform, the blind who could see and the lame who could walk; that despite the continuous loss of blood the padre lived on only a handful of meal each day. He told them the story of the American pilot who was all set to bomb the village when a vision of a bearded monk appeared on his wingtip and directed him away—and the pilot wasn't even Catholic. He told them that every time the monk said mass and elevated the Host, Christ Himself appeared in a vision on the altar, to those who could see such things, of course. For a few years Joe became something of a celebrity himself in Furnass because of his stories, which certainly did nothing to hurt business when he and Frank opened their men's store.

The thing was, the way Joe talked made it sound as though he had become friends with the monk and had taken a lot of special photographs of him. But in truth the only pictures Joe had of the padre were those he bought at the monastery gift shop, a fact that threatened to come out now that other people in town had traveled to Italy since the war and had seen the monk (and visited the monastery gift shop) for themselves. As for being friends with the monk, Joe had gone only once to the monastery, and the church that day was too crowded for him to get into. Joe stood with the faithful along the path back to the monk's cell, hoping for at least a glimpse of the padre after mass. When the monk finally came along, stumbling painfully on his bleeding feet, he stopped in front of Joe and amid a crush of wailing women looked straight at him—a boy of nineteen, standing there in his American serviceman's uniform—and said to him, Joe was almost certain, "Did the Yankees winna the pennant this year?" Joe shrugged, he didn't know, and the padre hobbled on. Over the years everyone else in the parish had given up on actually seeing Joe's pictures of the monk; there was always some reason why Joe couldn't show them right then, something else he always had to do to get the pictures ready or arranged or something. But the new priest, when Joe had trotted out his padre stories, took him at face value.

"You are aware, I'm sure, Joseph, that Holy Mother Church takes a guarded view of such phenomena as stigmatics," Father Mulroy was saying. "There are always some emotional types who might get carried away. True faith must always be based on Reason. . . ."

Joe, sitting now at the counter of the Furnass Grill, giggled. He had walked away from the priest, simply turned his back and walked on down the steps to his car and drove away; for all he knew Father Mulroy was still standing there talking. Joe giggled again, more like a snort. The little Capuchin was back, this time on the orange juice dispenser, posed on the faucet as if standing on a tightrope.

"Giuseppe, Giuseppe, why have you forsaken me?"

"Padre, I've been wanting to ask you the same question."

Joe raised his hand in benediction to the little priest. Jo the waitress, who happened to be walking past, crossed herself.

"Thanks Joe, I needed that. While you're at it, how about blessing the sweet rolls too, they're a little stale this morning. . . ."

Joe left some money on the counter—one dollar or ten, he wasn't sure—and slogged out the door and down the street, squinting against the autumn sunlight. In the window of the Little People Shop, Whitey crawled about on his hands and knees, wrestling the sleeves of a new winter coat onto the arms of a mannequin of a naked child; when he saw Joe, Whitey grinned and waved and gave the thumbs-up salute. Well, so much for what he *didn't* tell Whitey last night. Now Joe wondered what he *did* tell him.

After unlocking the front door and turning off the burglar alarm and turning on the overhead fluorescents, Joe walked the length of Peregrini Brothers, pulling off dustcovers, opening display cabinets, turning on spotlights. At the rear of the store, he sized up the figure of the plump, graying, aging man in the full-length three-way mirror (good suit, though). Then he pushed the center panel open a crack and groped one-armed along the shelf inside the storeroom, cheek by jowl with the other Joe in the mirror; by touch he found the right hatbox—an Adam's Pacesetter, size seven and a half—and took out a bottle of Christian Brothers brandy. He took a large mouthful, swishing it around his teeth like a mouthwash before swallowing it, took a couple more swallows for good measure, and returned the bottle. After digging his breath mints from his pocket, he hung his suit coat in the storeroom; as the mirrored panel closed behind him, he had a brief three-sided view of himself—reflections upon reflections into infinity—before he turned away. He flatfooted back to the cash register midway down the length of the long narrow store and sat up on the edge of the counter, swinging his legs like a schoolboy.

"So this is your store, eh Giuseppe? Very nice, very modern. How do you like it?"

"I'm very proud of it," Joe said, somewhat surprised to be asked the question.

The padre smiled and nodded. He was standing on a little cloud in front of the Hush Puppies, the vision extending all the way from the six and a half Ds to the eleven Es. Small, childlike angels fluttered about his head—the monk had to brush them away occasionally like pesky flies—and behind him was a glimpse of a gentle landscape of rolling hills. The marks of the stigmata on his hands and feet glowed like stoplights. As Joe watched, the padre floated around the store, examining the racks of Botany suits and Harris Tweed sport coats, the display cases of McGregor sweaters and Arrow shirts. Joe was afraid that later he'd find a trail of blood over everything.

"That means a lot to me, Padre, that you like it. But why did you ask me if I liked it?"

"Oh, I was just wondering, that's all." The little monk smiled sadly, as if he knew a secret. "Wondering if it was worth it. . . ."

"Worth what?" Joe laughed a little.

"Worth what you had to give up."

"What did I have to give up? You make it sound like there's almost something wrong with running a store. There isn't, is there?"

"No, no, of course not. There are some people who like it very much. It is their bliss."

"Well, ha ha, it's certainly not my bliss or anything like that. Dealing with people is a real pain. Half the time you have to convince them to want something just to get rid of them. But customers don't stand a chance against a super-salesman like me."

Joe gave him his best salesman's smile—he used to practice it in front of a mirror when they first opened the store so he'd get it right—an expression he always likened proudly to that of a smiling shark. The vision of the monk only cocked his head and looked at him; he adjusted his footing on his cloud, sending little showers of rain over a rack of belts.

"But now that you mention it, there was something once that I really liked to do." Joe went on, growing more animated. "The summer before I went into the army I worked in a little welding shop down on First Avenue. I think that was the happiest time of my life. I really liked welding, fusing two pieces of metal together into one, watching the bead as you went along, being careful not to lose your puddle of molten metal—it was exciting. And I liked working with my hands, having something when you're done that you can sit back and look at. I was pretty good at it too, old man Harriman said I was a natural."

"You couldn't get a job as a welder when you came back from the war?"

"Well, Frank really wanted this place and I hated to disappoint him. And welding's a dirty job, you know? And you can't get anywhere with it, you can't be somebody. Frank and me are important people in this town because of this store, we're one of the leading merchants. Of course, that meant more before the mills started closing, but still. . . . Yes sir, this place's been good to me, and it's easy, a lot of the time I only stand around, I'm very comfortable. . . ."

"Giuseppe, Giuseppe. . . .

"What? Tell me."

"Joe, Joe . . ."

The vision became brother Frank standing in front of him, bent over slightly so he could peer into Joe's eyes. When Joe finally focused on him, he screamed and jumped off the counter. "Don't do that!"

"My, we are in a bad way today, aren't we?" Frank smiled.

Frank was nearly as thick as he was wide, a block of a man who moved through a room benevolently, as if he could destroy it at any time but chose not to. The impression was tempered (or perhaps enhanced) by a smile that appeared shoulder-wide; it was that smile—calm, self-assured, amiable, unflappable—that always got to Joe the most. He had grown up with that smile smiling over him, whenever his older brother, out of anger or whim or whatever, chose to sit on his chest. It was the smile that later on in life looked down on him every day from the balcony of the store as Frank sat up in the office happily figuring accounts. Now Frank pawed the floor a couple of times, clapped his hands together, and readjusted his smile—his standard gestures when he didn't know what to say.

"Well, how did it go last night?" he said finally.

"Oh, you know, as well as a thing like that can."

"Whitey took the news okay?"

"Yes, he seemed to take it okay."

"Good, good. I thought it would sound better coming from you," Frank said, rubbing his hands together. "Whitey has to understand that business is business. We simply can't afford to pass up a deal like this to sell the building. With the mill closings, we'll probably never have another opportunity. And we're not getting any younger."

"He has to understand."

"Like we always said, you're the charm and I'm the brains."

"That's me. Mr. Charm."

The two brothers, having exhausted their possibilities for conversation, stood there as in a frieze, looking at each other for who knows how long until Whitey and Midge came through the front door and bustled back to the counter. The couple was all smiles.

"We wanted to come over and thank you personally, Frank-buddy," Whitey said, shaking his hand.

"Thank me?" Frank said.

Midge planted a sloppy kiss on his cheek. "A new five-year lease, with a guaranteed no increase in rent! Why, it's more than we ever dreamed of. We can never thank you enough."

"I woke her up as soon as I got home last night to tell her what Joe said," Whitey said. "I'll tell you the truth, we were scared silly, when Joe asked me out for a drink like that, weren't we Midge?"

"Well, what do you expect? We heard all these rumors in town about a big new building going up and talk that you were thinking of selling this building and all. But I said the Peregrini brothers wouldn't do such a thing and leave their old friends out in the cold just to turn a buck. Oh, you dear man, now we can plan all sorts of things for our store. . . ."

Frank looked at Joe. Joe shrugged, gave brother Frank his best salesman's smile, and forgetting that he was only in his shirtsleeves, walked out the door.

He drove around town for a while, up and down the steep streets, avoiding the street where he lived, then headed toward the Lower End; he cruised slowly along River Street, the Street of the Seven Oaks as it was known when he was a kid, past the old lock and dam. Across the Allehela the bluffs of the valley's hills pushed the horizon up out of sight; trees marked the top of the sandstone cliffs like the red and yellow flags of an encircling army. He drove on, along Bridge Street then under Ohio River Boulevard, past the Furnass Builders Supply yard, the new sewage treatment plant, a small run-down park leading to the water's edge. The road got narrower and bumpier as it neared the tall concrete viaduct that sealed off the end of the valley; beyond the arch of the viaduct, the road was nothing more than a dirt lane. He passed a row of vandalized picnic shelters; the docks of the boat club closed for winter; the remains of a shack. The bare trees and scrub brush scraped along the sides of his car. He continued slowly under the railroad trestle and out to the promontory of land at the point where the smaller river emptied into the Ohio.

He hadn't been here in years, not since he and Frank played here as kids; he circled around in the gravel and stopped. Standing by itself on the river's edge was an abutment for a bridge torn down long ago, an abandoned stone tower thirty feet high. The sandstone was black from the years of smoke and dirt from the mills; the surface of the abutment, all the way to the top, was covered with names, scratched into the surface or painted with spray cans. In front of the abutment was a small tree of heaven; the leaves were gone but the branches bore a pair of soiled Jockey shorts and several used condoms. On the river, a diesel tug pushed its load of coal barges upstream toward Pittsburgh, its engines throbbing, pulsing as if they beat inside his head. Joe rested his elbow on the windowsill and patted his fingertips against his mouth.

"I'm trying, Padre. I hope you know I'm really trying."

"I suppose you are, in your own way." The monk sat beside him in the car facing the river. "You are gentle, Giuseppe. Perhaps too gentle."

"You liked me, didn't you, Padre? That time you looked at me in the crowd outside the monastery. I always thought you liked me."

"I waited for you."

"You stopped that time because you saw something in me, am I right?"

"Yes. I can see something still." The Capuchin turned toward Joe, stretched his arm with the bleeding hand across the back of the seat.

"It's a vocation, isn't it? I always thought I had the calling to be a priest."

"Not exactly, Giuseppe."

"Then tell me, Padre. What is it?"

"What I see, Giuseppe, is that you are lost."

"Lost? Me? How can I be lost? I grew up in this part of town. You're the one who's a stranger around here, ha ha."

He laughed, but he was the only one laughing. He looked, but he was the only one there.

. . . Crow, crow, have you any songs for me? From somewhere off in the woods to his right there is a clacking sound, like someone beating two rocks together. A glastig perhaps? The King of the Crows calling to him? Duncan angles over in that direction, still behind Hugh Campbell but sweeping off to the side, away from the other. He tramps through the ferns, comes to the edge of a hollow, sloping away from him down through the forest. The slope is covered with fallen leaves, a thin carpet of red and yellow, the mirror image of the leaves overhead. In one of the trees, a heavy branch has at some time been half-torn from the trunk in a storm, the broken branch fallen and resting now against another. In the wind high overhead, the broken branch moves against the other, a repeated clack. He's not even disappointed at this point that that's all it is. His disillusionment is already complete.

It's foolish and pointless to be looking for things that aren't here. There are no spirits or signs. Here or anywhere else. There is nothing from another world trying to help him or get a message to him. He's not one of the special ones. It's only been his imaginings. His feelings of abandonment and loss are complete by this time too. Whatever gave way in him that morning at Bushy Run has worked its way through his mind until he no longer has faith or hope in anything. After searching for so long for signs and bogles from another world, after finding only the bogles and savageries within his own inner world, he no longer trusts anything, or anyone, in this world.

Why is this Campbell so intent on leading him deeper into the woods? The Campbells at Glencoe woke in the middle of the night to kill their hosts, the MacDonalds. Does this grenadier have something of the sort in mind for him? Duncan doesn't know what to believe anymore, whom he can trust. He just wants to live through this, to get back to the others safely. The two men are walking twenty yards or so abreast of each other. Hugh Campbell waves at him between the trees, motions for Duncan to come back, to stay closer to him. Duncan reluctantly edges over in that direction, but he's cautious, taking his time.

As the two men angle toward each other, the forest in front of them appears to be coming to an end. It's light through the trees as if they are approaching a cliff, a drop-off at the end of the world. High above in the vault of leaves there's a noisy rustling. A crow tries to land on a branch much too small for it. The bird beats its wings among the leaves, sending a shower of leaves down on the two men below. The crow calls raucously, almost as if it were laughing. Duncan glances up at the bird but he's more interested in what's in front of him. The forest is gone. All the trees for a hundred yards are lying on the ground, knocked over all in a row. A great swath cut in the forest, extending across the entire valley, down the hill on this side to the river and up the other side. The roots of the trees are pulled up naked and exposed, twisted like ganglia, like guts and entrails ripped open to the air. A few yards into the felled trees are the sheep they've been looking for, penned in on three sides by a tangle of fallen branches. The animals look at them, expectant, frightened.

"So here's the wee daft beasties," Duncan says and starts across the open. He stops cold when he hears Hugh Campbell behind him pull back the hammer on his flintlock. . . .

DOWN BY THE RIVER

1972

He should have brought a jacket. Here along the bank of the river it was cooler than he expected, cooler than when he left the store. But he didn't want to go back to the car now. All he had with him anyway was his sport coat. Al continued along the rough trail. No, he wasn't prepared for this at all. The bare branches of sumac and trees of heaven whipped his arms in the short-sleeve white shirt. He was winded already, his breath gone short. He loosened his tie; his sweating made him even colder. But what did he expect? It had been thirty-five years—and now he was pushing around thirty-five extra pounds, most of it hanging off his stomach—since he'd been out like this, hiked somewhere like this. He needed to walk more, he knew that. He pressed on. His camera dangled from his wrist like a charm.

There was the sound of the water at the falls near the old lock; the hiss of traffic on the bridge behind him leading back to town. The cry of a distant crow. Otherwise it was quiet here, all the sounds faraway. Even his footsteps scuffing along the dirt path. Hushed, as if the world held its breath. Desolate. As was fitting, he supposed. Considering what happened here. Part of why it happened here. It could be no other way.

He had never been here before, across the river from the town. Fifty years old and he had never been this close to the river before. Growing up in the town, he had been taught to stay away from the river. Besides the obvious danger, it was a place where nice people didn't go. Bad things supposedly went on by the river, something to do with vagrants and bums and the dangerous poor. That he was doing this now, taking off in the middle of the day like this, was exciting, something almost forbidden, an adventure. Maybe his life was finally starting to change, open up. He grinned to himself, felt an extra bounce in his step. Along the path, low brambles tugged at his pants legs. Across the river, the town, the mills and factories, the valley's hills, spread along the opposite bank as if on a great stage. Both setting and audience for what happened here.

Foam, acrid and fecal-like, lapped along the edge of the river. There were old tires half in the water, half out; plastic bottles bobbing in the froth. Disgusting. From a distance he never would have believed it. A condom hanging from a bush. A kind of trophy? Good for you, friend. No, he shouldn't say that. Suppose his own daughter, Marcy. . . . Beyond the embankment he could see a line of roofs tucked back in a hollow, conjoined company housing from the days when they burned coke here. A few shacks—there was no other name for them—farther up the steep wooded hillside. Who would choose to live here, with the town just across the river? Rough people, no doubt, poor. Like hill people. Well, it was the tip of Appalachia, one step away, if that. Crushing poverty. They said the little girl—what was her name? Janice something—lived nearby. Take away civilization and that's what you get. He looked around uneasily. Kept walking.

The strip of land between the embankment and the river widened as the train tracks curved closer to the valley wall. The path split into two; through the brush and bare trees ahead, he could see the trails dividing again. A glimpse of a pond, stagnant water;

farther on, another. A maze of wetlands and straggly growth. None of it looked at all like the map they printed in the paper. The images on television. There had been a row of emergency vehicles, local and state police cars, the red and blue lights on their roofs flicking ineffectively in the sunlight. Clusters of men standing around talking among themselves. The colorful fall foliage, sumac and ironweed and chokecherry. Dappled sunlight sprocketing down. Then the small group of men coming down a slope, back through the trees. Making their way through the underbrush. Lifting the black rubber sack so it didn't drag on the ground. The remains in the sack light enough that it only took two of the men to carry it.

He continued along the web of trails. Keeping the river in sight as much as possible through the trees. The steep wall of the valley rising over all, sandstone and granite bluffs. Something had happened here during the French and Indian War, Al began to recall. A hazardous river crossing or some such thing, Highland soldiers passing through, later building a blockhouse where the town is now. A long way from home. A long way to come in those days, to die. In a strange wilderness. Alone. And Indians. Delaware and Shawnee and Mingo. The stories. They flayed their captives alive here on the riverbank, in view of the outpost on the other side. The screams of the women for days over the water. Hard to believe now. A history of violence to this place. Does the land remember? Did it attract violence now in memory from another time? Or was it always here? The forest primeval. Prime Evil.

Why did he come here? What did he think he'd find? He'd never done anything like this before, chase after a crime scene. As if to justify himself, he took the camera and tried to frame a few images. But there was nothing to focus on. All was a jumble of bare branches, dry twigs. Across the river, beyond the veil of cattails and dry grass lining the bank, the life of the town went on, irrespective of what happened here. She probably saw the town in her last moments, was aware that help was that close. And that it would not come. That no one would help her. Perhaps on that very day, at that very instant, he had stepped outside his shop, his shoe store on the main street, had looked at this very spot across the river. But he knew the world was cruel, uncaring, that didn't surprise him. That wasn't it—Wait, there was someone among the trees.

Out of the corner of his eye, for the briefest instant, he thought he saw something. Someone. Off the trail, in the scruffy undergrowth. He looked again, but there was no one there. He laughed at himself. Great. That's all he needed. To start seeing things. He turned inland, through the low brush, up a small rise, though he could still hear the river behind him. Something flashed, chirred through the branches, close to his head. He ducked; well, it seemed close. A mourning dove sat on a low branch a few yards ahead of him. He laughed again, this time out loud, in case anyone had seen him. (Who could see him?) The bird blinked stupidly at him, muttered something, then flew on through the woods, squeaking as it flapped as if its wings were loose on their hinges. He climbed a little farther, using the spindly trees for handholds, up onto a shelf of land. He was sweating, puffing hard. In the climb he had cut his hand, there were drops of blood on the front of his shirt. Great, now Gretchen would be on him when he got home. Something else. He sucked at the web at the base of his thumb, the blood metallic in his mouth. No, there was someone there.

A man stood in the tall grass at the edge of the trees. Dressed in brown duck work clothes, long jacket and matching pants like buckskin, and a quilted mechanic's hat. In the crook of his arm was a shotgun.

"You startled me," Al said. Aware that his voice cracked. "I didn't expect to find anyone around here."

The man at the edge of the trees, the grass up to his thighs—
he was the color of the dead grass and the bare trees—looked as
if he didn't expect to find anyone here either.

"I guess this is where it happened, huh? Somewhere around
here?" Al said it as a question but the man didn't say anything.
Only shifted the shotgun on his arm.

"Terrible thing," Al said, kicking at some grass near his feet.
His shoes were covered with leaves as if he'd been attacked by
leeches. "Terrible. I guess some kids found her, nobody usually
comes up this way. Sheriff said they might never have found her
otherwise."

"You a photographer?" the man finally spoke.

Al held up the point-and-shoot camera, dangling from his
wrist like a torn appendage. "Me? No, I just brought it along. I
don't know why. . . ."

The man pulled a piece of long-stemmed grass from its
sheath and stuck it in his mouth; the tasseled end fluttered as he
chewed on it. Studying Al, head cocked to one side. As if taking
his measure. His face was long and weathered, leathery, the face
of a man who spent most of his life out of doors. Al wished he
could still see the river. This place seemed too much out of the
way.

"Who'd want to rape a little girl, and then bash her head in
like that?" Al said.

"Is that what they think happened? That he raped her too?"

"Well, that's what everybody thinks must've happened."

"Can't they tell for sure?"

"I guess it's pretty hard. There wasn't much left of her, after
all that time."

The man spit the stem of grass from his mouth.

"Why would anybody want to do a terrible thing like that?"
Al said.

The man started to turn away, then stopped. "Why would anybody want to come all the way out here just to see where it happened? Maybe take a picture of it?"

"Well, what're you doing up here anyway?"

The man looked at him for a moment, and continued to move away. Began to blend in with the grass and the trees.

"Hey, what's your name, fellow?" Al called after him. "You live around here?"

As the man reached a group of trees he looked back over his shoulder. Al remembered his camera, put it to his eye. In the framed, lucid world of the viewfinder, the man appeared almost to smile when he saw what Al was doing. He turned around to face the camera; then raised the shotgun to his shoulder and aimed it at Al in return.

Al slowly lowered the camera. "I didn't take it," he said.

The man continued to sight down the barrel at him. When he finally lowered the gun there was a look of satisfaction on the other's face that sent a chill deep through Al. It was the look of a hunter after he's taken his shot, after he's made his kill. He was looking at Al as if Al were already dead.

For a moment the other held the gun at waist level and waved the end of the barrel slowly in Al's direction. As if he were tracing Al's outline with it. Defining him in some way. Then he disappeared on into the woods.

Al stared at the place where the man had been. He was trembling, his clothes were sweated through. When he came to himself again, he turned and ran back through the brush, back down the slope, crashing and slipping and stumbling as he tried to find the trail again, running toward the river, tried to find the way back again, back the way he came.

. . . He whirls around. Hugh stands at the edge of the trees, aiming his musket at him. Before Duncan can say anything, Hugh fires but misses. The ball whizzes by him, wide by several feet. Then the grenadier throws down the musket and draws his broadsword and rushes at him, screaming "Cruachan!" Duncan raises his own musket and fires point-blank. Hugh tumbles backward, moans on the ground, then is still. Everything is still. Duncan stands holding the musket, breathing heavily, trembling. His throat is dry, suddenly he's very thirsty. What happened here? The bloody crazy Campbell. . . . Then there's a sound behind him. Duncan whirls back. Standing beside the uprooted trunk of a tree is an Indian. His bare skin covered with grease glistens in the strong sunlight in the clearing. He is wearing only a loincloth and tall buckskin leggings up to his thighs. His head is shaved with a tuft of black hair sticking up on top; his eyes are circled with black and vermilion, with black streaks zigzagging down his cheeks. For a long moment the Indian looks quizzically at him. Duncan is frozen, he can't move. Hugh must have seen the Indian from where he was, where Duncan couldn't. The shot wasn't meant for him at all. But Duncan still can't move. Then a slow smile awakens on the Indian's face, a growing look of comprehension. He grunts something and steps forward, lowering his rifle, grinning at Duncan. He eases, sidesteps around him, still not completely sure, toward Hugh. He says something, the only word of which Duncan recognizes is "brother." The Indian says it again, makes a gesture between himself and Duncan. Then the Indian relaxes completely, walks over freely to where Hugh lies on the ground. He kneels beside him, prods him a little, then turns the Highlander over on his stomach. He looks at Duncan and mutters something again, is happy as if he and Duncan share something. Laying his rifle aside, the Indian slips off the knife

hanging from a thong around his neck. Carefully, almost tenderly, with terrible efficiency, the Indian takes a handful of Hugh's fine reddish-yellow hair and begins to cut. Slips the blade under the base of the hair as blood oozes over the blade. The patch of exposed skull under Hugh's scalp is whiter than anything human should ever be. . . .

THE GIRL WITH THE NUT-BROWN HAIR

1977

One

At first she thought it must be Ron knocking around somewhere in the apartment. Debbie looked at the clock on the nightstand; later the red numerals would glow forever in the darkness of her memories: 1:48. She couldn't believe he wasn't there—that was one thing she could say about Ron at least, he was always there—she even called out, "Ron?" before she realized it was someone knocking at the front door. It was Wally, his partner.

"It's Ron," he said, not looking at her, staring at the doorframe somewhere near her knee. She wanted to grab him and scream at him, Look at me, damn it, you're supposed to look at me when you tell me something like this. You've looked at me enough times before. "There's been an accident."

"But what are you doing here, he wasn't on duty. . . ."

"They called me when they recognized who it was. Jesus, what was he doing driving around at this time of night. . . ?"

She threw on jeans and her aerobic shoes and a red flannel pullover and let Wally drive her to the hospital. It didn't occur to Debbie to ask if Ron's parents had been informed, she assumed Miriam, his mother, knew already, the way she always knew everything else that went on in their lives. At the upper end of the main street, at the bottom of the hill on Orchard Avenue, they passed the scene of the accident, illuminated by sputtering flares and the pulsing emergency lights on the patrol cars and fire trucks. A fireman with a push broom swept up mounds of broken glass, mangled strips of chrome. There was a dark spot on the pavement: oil, or Ron's blood? A tow truck was winching the remains of the black Firebird up onto the wrecker's flatbed; the front end of the car was pushed back into the passenger compartment, the remainder of the car was crimped in the middle, wrung like a washcloth. Wally told her that Ron had been speeding down the hill and lost control at the curve at the bottom, plowing into a utility pole.

"He must have really been flying," Wally said, marveling.

"At least the car was clean."

Wally looked puzzled; Debbie shook her head to say Forget it.

"He must have been crazy," were Wally's last words on the subject.

Crazy with rage at me, she thought. That night she never meant for Ron to go out and get himself killed; she only meant for him to go out and get the car washed.

"All I said was, 'You didn't get the car washed,'" she told him.

"No, you didn't. You said, 'You *still* didn't get the car washed,' like you're accusing me or something. Look, I worked twelve hours today, I'm whipped. I didn't have time."

"Okay, so forget it. So the car rusts out and we don't get our money out of it. I just don't see the sense of having a nice car if you're not going to take care of it."

Ron stood in the doorway, a can of Iron City in his hand, watching her. It was after eleven thirty, he had just gotten home from his shift. He was standing between the two rooms, a silhouette, backlit by the fluorescents over the sink in the kitchen; his face was part of the darkness of the room where she was. She tucked her legs further up under her on the couch, her toes peeking out from the edge of the nightgown; she shrugged and pulled a face and looked back at the television at a rerun of *Three's Company*. After seven years of marriage she knew how to get at him.

"Oh for fuck's sake! All right, I'll go wash the goddamn car," he said finally, turned and flung his beer can across the kitchen. The can clattered against the cabinets beside the refrigerator and pinballed down among the metal legs of the dinette. Tomorrow, Dotty, her downstairs neighbor, curious as ever, would undoubtedly ask Debbie about it: "Did you drop something in the kitchen last night, hon?"

The tricky part then was to get him out the door before he turned on her—to hit her or fuck her, at this point it wouldn't matter which, it would be the same. He had been working plainclothes lately; under his nylon shell was the bulge of his shoulder holster. She thought Maybe someday he'll take it out and shoot me and end both our misery. He stood in the doorway, a silhouette, hands on his hips, legs spread, ready, waiting for her to say something. Anything that would enable him to stay, or provoke him enough that he would come across the room after her. I won't even give him that satisfaction. She kept her eyes on the TV until she heard the front door slam and knew he was gone. Gone: to an extent she never could have imagined.

It wasn't as if it was such a terrible thing to ask. Some nights he went out on his own at this hour, without her prodding him, to wash the car, the nights when he came off duty and couldn't sleep, the nights when there had been trouble on his shift, a fight or a shooting. Or the nights when they made love and she wouldn't do what he wanted her to, when she wouldn't go down on him or let him turn her over facedown. Washing the car at the Pay-'N-Spray seemed to relax him. Tonight, however, she had thought she'd wait up for him; she smiled to herself, unfolded her legs, turned off the TV, and did a little dance, pointy-toed, across the room, arms outstretched, trailing the flimsy stuff of the nightgown behind her. But she was asleep when the knock came.

Two

Nothing in her life prepared her for what she found at the hospital. Nothing could have. At the hospital she entered a new world, a world she only vaguely knew existed. A world self-contained, self-perpetuating in a way, with its own priorities and hierarchies and customs. That only distantly reflected the world beyond the soft swing of its pneumatic doors. A sterile world in whites and pastels, a world of starched linen and blips on a monitor and hushed alarms. Full of the perfume of antiseptics to cover the smells of illness and decay and death. A world that, however unreal it seemed with its controlled temperatures and unrelenting lights, however removed from the rest of the world behind its sealed windows and curtains on metal rails pulled closed around a bed, would soon overwhelm her own world until it became her only reality. A world that drained the energy from her, as if the struggle going on within the building to maintain life sapped the strength of anyone healthy who stepped inside.

And she was introduced to a new husband, or rather, a new kind of husband. Ron had become a lump under a pile of bedclothes, attached to tubes putting liquids into him and tubes taking liquid out of him, tubes to give him air to breathe and wires to monitor the amount of life left in him. The first time she saw him, when they finally let her in the room after eighteen hours of waiting—she stood on tiptoe to get a better view, what with the tubes in his mouth and up his nose, the bruises and the swellings; his face was exposed but his head was wrapped like the headdress of a nun—she didn't know him at all.

"Can he hear me?" she asked the young doctor who stood beside her. "Does he even know I'm here?"

"We don't know. We don't think so. He doesn't respond to any verbal commands or physical stimuli, and there's no increase of activity on the monitors, so we can assume he doesn't—"

"We?"

"Pardon?"

"You keep saying 'we,' like there's a whole bunch of you or something. I only see one guy standing here with me."

She did see him too, perhaps too well. Dr. Cartwright looked the way a young doctor was supposed to, with black wavy hair and a jaw that could punch through walls and soft lowering eyes. Brown eyes; she thought he'd be gentle in bed. And hated herself for thinking such a thing: here she was, standing at the bedside of her potato-clock husband, thinking of coming on to another guy. Did young Dr. Cartwright know what she was thinking?

"You've been under a terrible amount of stress since last night," Dr. Cartwright said. "Why don't you come out now and we'll talk later when we know more. . . ."

He put his arm around her—she would always love him for that—as he guided her out between the curtains around the bed and down the aisle of the ICU. She could feel his body, his solidness, beneath the white lab coat. She wanted him and hated the wanting and thought she'd always be a slut.

Ron's mother and father were in the waiting room, as they had been almost since the time Debbie got there last night; and Wally was there, of course, good old faithful Wally. Miriam was incensed that the wife was able to see her son before the mother.

"I want to see him, Doctor. I have to see my boy."

"I'm afraid nobody can see him anymore right now, he needs his rest. As I'm sure all you folks do too. He's out of immediate danger for the time being, and we have no way of knowing how long it will take for him to regain consciousness. Or if he will regain consciousness. Why don't you all take this opportunity to go home and get some rest and come back later. We'll call you if there's any change."

"I don't have a car now," Debbie said to no one in particular, realizing the fact for the first time. "I don't know how I'm going to get back and forth."

Miriam looked away. Eddie, Ron's father—a shorter heavier version of his son, complete with mustache and failing chin—started to say something, then thought better of it.

"I'll make sure you get here, until we can get you another car," Wally said.

"Thanks for thinking of me, Eddie," Debbie said to her father-in-law. "You almost had enough guts to go against her that time."

Eddie blushed; Miriam sputtered; Dr. Cartwright lowered his eyes. Debbie left them standing there and headed down the hall, uncertain herself whether she wanted to laugh or cry. Wally hurried to catch up; he started to put his arm around her, as the doctor had done, then stopped himself. They didn't say anything until they got to the parking lot.

"Don't you think you're being a little hard on them?"

"You don't know them like I do. That old sow will try to eat Ron alive, now that he's helpless and can't defend himself. Look what she's done to her husband."

Wally held the car door for her and waited till she got situated. He filled the doorframe, eclipsing the afternoon, the bulk of an ex–high school lineman if not the muscle tone. "Maybe the world will look better to you after you get some rest."

The same words she had said to him once. In a parking lot in Pittsburgh after the two of them had driven there for dinner so no one would recognize them. Snow fell steadily around them, defining the cones of light bearing down from the spotlights on the roof of the building; in the hushed snowy evening the only sounds were the distant music from inside the restaurant, a car in the next block spinning its wheels. Snow dusted his hair, tangled in the strands before melting away, as he held the car door for her.

"Poor Wally, you look so sad. We probably shouldn't have tried this."

"Why wouldn't I look sad? I'm married and in love with my best friend's wife."

"But nothing happened, Wally. And it won't happen, you know that. Maybe the world will look better to you after you get some rest."

"It would take a miracle to make the world look better," he had said.

She thought to use the same words now, but decided not to remind him.

Three

He had beat her at times, but she couldn't blame him. She would have beat herself, if she could, pounded the daylights out of herself. The first time it was almost play. It was shortly after they were married, she had changed her clothes after work and was doing a few stretches on the living room floor when Ron came out of the bedroom and stood over her. "Whatcha doing down there?"

"This is as far as I got. I'll go out and get us something to eat in a minute."

She raised her feet off the floor, brought her knees to her chest and held them there, curled into herself. She was aware that Ron was watching her, watching her bottom in the pink sweat pants; she wiggled her upturned ass to tease him, spread her knees apart to show him her crotch, then saw his expression change from curiosity and amusement to one of interest. Before she could bring her legs down again Ron dropped to his knees and held her in that position.

"We've never done it this way before."

"No, my neck's got a crick in it." Thinking he still wasn't serious about it. Thinking she could still get out of it. She laughed.

He laughed too, but he tried to spread her knees apart.

"Hey!" she laughed again, meaning Don't!

But she couldn't hold her knees together against him, he was too strong; he forced her knees apart and then lifted her legs until she was spread with her ankles resting on his shoulders, his crotch pressed against her as he dry-humped her a couple of times. Then he started pulling off her sweat pants, exposing her ass and thighs. She grabbed at the pants.

"Ron, come on. I'm tired, that's enough."

"And I'm horny, and there's never enough. This'll be fun. Something new."

"No," she said and gripped her pants firmly enough to stop him.

"Let go, Debbie."

She struggled to pull her pants back on, wriggling to try to get her legs down off his shoulders. "Ron, let me up!"

She tried to laugh; he laughed too, at her struggles. Then she got frightened and frantic and pushed at him and tried harder to pull her legs down and took a swipe at his face and he slapped her, hard across the cheek. For a moment they both stopped. Ron stared down at her, as startled as she was that he had done it. Then in the calm between them, he slapped her again.

"If you didn't want me to fuck you, why the hell did you show me your goddamn ass?"

And he hit her again, back and forth across the face with the flat of his hand, and when she wouldn't let go of her pants he hit her in the mouth with his fist, and again, then wrenched off her pants and rammed into her as she cried, thinking He's right, I deserve this.

It was over soon enough that evening, but the slapping and punching had only begun. There were times over the years of their marriage, covering the bruises with makeup or inventing another story about bumping into something, when she didn't care whether Ron lived or died; there were times now, thinking back over what their marriage had been, when she felt she was the one who was brain-dead.

"You can't let yourself get down," Wally said one night at the hospital when she told him how she felt. It had been months now with Ron in a coma; they met there at his bedside each evening like it was a rite. "You can't think about what might have been."

"But how can I go on living when he's just lying here?"

"Because that's what people do. Because that's what it's all about. Going on."

"Is that what you learned, being a cop?"

She meant it as a slap to be hurtful, but Wally shrugged it off. No, she thought, that's a silly question. He's learning it now. He's learning it by having to go on with his life while his best friend is lying there, he's learning it by trying not to be in love with me now that he actually could be. It was like Wally to try to buck up her spirits—it was a given that he came to the hospital as much to see her as to see Ron. But the things he pointed out to her, she had already come to see for herself.

She grew up in another valley mill town along the river a few miles away, a town like this town, cast from the same mold, but she had never felt at home in Furnass during their years of marriage, a feeling compounded by, among other things, old football rivalries. It was Ron's town, even though she worked in the bank here when she first met him, Ron the Policeman, worked at the bank still; he had insisted they live here, a few blocks from his parents'. But gradually over the months, with Ron out of the picture, she began to eke out a new life for herself. When the insurance check finally came through, Debbie went out and bought a car of her own—a Buick Skylark (Ron hated Buicks), bright red (Ron always said red was too hot in the summer)—so she was no longer dependent on anyone, not even Wally. She learned how to take care of herself, better than before she met Ron; she learned how to use her best features, learned how to dress well (Ron had never let her spend the money), learned how to do her makeup, changed her hairstyle from the child-like curly-perm to a stylish shag-cut; she learned how to carry herself, talk to people when there wasn't a teller cage between them (Ron would have accused her of being pushy or flirting or worse). It had become her town, without her even realizing it. She had become herself.

Four

One night when she arrived at the hospital it was obvious that Ron hadn't been bathed for a day or so—the odor was apparent as soon as she walked into the room. None of the nurses had time right then, so Debbie found a basin and washcloth and began to wash him herself. Over the nine months of being in the hospital, Ron had wasted away until he reminded her of pictures she had seen of victims in concentration camps; he felt now as if someone had tried to put a man together out of latex and mop handles. As she washed down around his crotch, she examined his poor shrunken pizzle stuck in the catheter, his shriveled balls. His genitalia had always been a mystery to her; she had rarely had the opportunity to examine them when they weren't aimed at her. Daintily, she held his stunted penis upright between her fingertips and flopped it back and forth a couple times. She was massaging his balls, amazed at the way the stones shifted back and forth in their sack, when Wally came in.

"Debbie, what are you doing?"

"I thought maybe this would feel good to him."

"Omigod, don't. You're going to kill him."

"What?" she looked at him across the bed, thinking maybe he was joking.

"It would be like somebody squeezing your ovaries."

"But I'm not hitting him or anything, I know that can really hurt a guy. I'm only rubbing them." She held them up and squeezed a testis from one sack to the other.

"Jeesus, I mean it, don't do that!" Wally grabbed his own crotch and crossed his legs in sympathy, pop-eyed. "Shit, it hurts even to think about it. Be-lieve me, the pain would be excruciating. Leave him alone."

Debbie felt awful. And embarrassed. She laid his balls down gently and covered Ron again, pulled down his hospital gown and adjusted the sheets over him. She and Wally looked at each other across the bed, across the emaciated figure lying between them; they looked at Ron's face to see if there was any reaction—he lay there as motionless, as emotionless, as ever, his face sunken in upon itself until he was barely recognizable—and back at each other. And dissolved into giggles.

"I was trying to do something nice for him," Debbie said, covering her mouth. Together they vented laughter like escaping steam.

"If that didn't get a reaction out of him, nothing will," Wally said, and got them started all over again. They tried to stifle their laughter but it only made it worse and they had to leave the room. In the hallway, they collapsed against each other, holding each other up, laughing hysterically. As she nestled against his chest, this bulwark of a man, she looked up at him, his fleshy cheeks moist with tears from laughing so hard, and thought, Why not? He loves me, he'd be good to me, we have fun together. Why not Wally?

Five

Ron had been in the coma more than a year and a half when Debbie called Dr. Cartwright and told him she had made her decision. The doctor met her at the nurses' station and, as they walked down the corridor, he took her arm as naturally as if they were lovers. Will we be lovers now? Debbie wondered. She could smell his aftershave, the surgical soap on his hands.

"I know we talked about it before, on several occasions," he said, his head inclined toward her, speaking softly. "I just want to make sure that this is what you want to do."

"Don't you think it's what I should do?"

She felt a momentary panic; the old insecurities rushed over her. Suppose Ron was lying there aware of everything that was going on but was unable to let them know he was in there, as if he were buried alive and his own body was both his grave and casket? Suppose every time she came into the room his heart sang? How could she know?

"No, Debbie, it's not for me to decide. I've already told you what I think. I'm confident that the only thing that's keeping him alive is the life-support system. There's absolutely no brain activity now, the EEG is flat, and I'm confident that as soon as the respirator is removed he'll simply stop. Quickly and quietly. I wouldn't tell you that if I thought there was one iota of a chance he might recover in any way or that his living functions might keep on without the support systems. But ultimately it's your decision."

She wondered: Would they become lovers now? After they killed Ron? It seemed only fitting in a way: to make final what had been lingering on between them, after they finally stopped Ron's lingering on. They walked down the hallway together to determine Ron's sentence, his judge and jury and executioners too. Her high heels clicked on the wax floors like the ticking of a clock. A bomb hidden in a package and tied with a pretty bow.

"I think it's time to remove the machines and let him go peacefully."

They stopped in front of Ron's door. Dr. Cartwright tilted his head to look at her, as if trying to read her heart through her eyes.

What does my heart tell you, good doctor? Debbie thought as she returned his gaze. What does my heart tell me?

"We didn't contact his parents," Dr. Cartwright said. "Are you sure you want to proceed without discussing it with them first?"

"It's my decision to make, isn't it? My responsibility?"

"Yes, certainly."

"Then I've made the decision."

"Do you think . . . they might want to be here. . . . ?"

"Yes, I suppose they would. But let's go ahead. They never let us have a life together when he was alive. At least I can be alone with Ron for the other. I think it's what Ron would want." No, it's what I want. Evil, evil heart.

He nodded, his lips compressed to a thin line, and held the door for her to go in. A nurse was waiting for them, and a technician. The mechanic of the crowd, Debbie thought. It's a wonder he doesn't wear coveralls, have a screwdriver sticking out of his back pocket. She wondered if he could fix her washing machine as well as turn off life-support systems; she wondered if she was going crazy. Debbie went over to the bed, looked at Ron a moment. He weighed less than a hundred pounds now, a skeleton marionette with the strings gone slack; she decided he might as well be already laid out in his casket, except that whoever did the makeup on his face had done a rotten job. Good-bye, Ron the Policeman. Ron the son-of-a-bitch. She tried to think of something kind and significant to wish him but couldn't come up with anything. She bent down and kissed his cheek. She tried not to liken it to kissing a waxed fruit; it was all she could do not to wipe her lips. As she stood there, his eyes suddenly opened, he looked at her, he raised up, sat up in bed, he was well again, he was Ron again, a miracle; but it didn't happen. It was time. She nodded to Dr. Cartwright, who nodded to the technician.

It was disturbingly simple. The technician standing behind the respirator looked down over the top of the machine, waved his hand over the control panel—it looked like a conjuring trick, but he was only trying to find the correct switch while looking at it upside down—and clicked it off, leaving in place for the time being the trachea and the electrodes and the IVs. The room was suddenly very quiet; she hadn't realized how accustomed she had become to the sound of the machine. She also hadn't realized how much the respirator blocked out the other noises of the hospital; there were the sounds of a cart rattling by in the corridor, people talking, laughing, a TV in another patient's room. It seemed unfeeling and cruel that life could be going on so normally beyond the door, while here in this room a fellow human being—her Ron—was dying.

She turned to look where the others were looking, at the monitor above the bed, at the blip moving across the measured green lines, waiting for it to stop, waiting for the singing straight line of light across the screen that would announce a life was over. As they watched the blip hesitated, faltered, grew weak, started to fade—the peaks and valleys evening out, the signs of life beginning to lessen—then caught, stuttered, paused, and resumed its pattern again, not quite as strong as before when the respirator was doing the breathing for him, but there nonetheless, flowing, tracing the topography of his heartbeat, continuous, alive. They waited a few minutes, a few minutes more. Dr. Cartwright took his stethoscope and listened to Ron's chest.

"I don't know," he said raising his head, looking at Debbie. He removed the stethoscope from his ears and yoked it around his neck. "Maybe he'll stop in the next hour, maybe in a day or so.

Maybe it'll take years. The way he sounds right now, I'd say it could be years."

Debbie ran from the room, sobbing, her hand to her mouth. Terrified.

Six

It was a false spring, no doubt. It was too early, February, for the real spring to be here already; the temperatures were in the seventies, the crocuses were poking up, the trees and bushes were greening oblivious to the dangers of frosts and late snows—but Debbie would take it. She sat on a bench in the park above the main street with its view of the town down the slope of the hill and the mills and the curve of the river, lifted her face to a sun as insubstantial as if wrapped in gauze, letting its near-warmth wash over her.

"Why did you decide to do this all of sudden?" Wally said.

"It's not all of a sudden, you know that. You even went with me a while ago to look at some larger places. And the hospital says I have to move him. They told me again this week. There's nothing more they can do for him. They said they're not in the nursing care business and that he needs someplace where he can get the right therapy. So. . . ."

He was struggling with it, she could tell. Dear Wally, she thought, peeking at him occasionally through gunslit eyes. She continued to keep her face to the sun; Wally stared straight ahead. They ate their sandwiches, watching a riverboat maneuver its string of barges toward the lock. Pushing at it like an ant at the back end of a too-long twig. As he tried to think of what to say next, Wally rolled something over and over on the fingertips of one hand, something too small to be seen. Dear sweet Wally.

"Do his parents know?"

"I don't know. I haven't told them, if that's what you mean. They'll find out when I move him. It's not their responsibility, and it's not their choice to make. They said they won't do anything to help pay for his long-term care, so as far as I'm concerned they're not part of the process."

"Maybe they can't do anything to help. Maybe they don't have the money. . . ."

"As if I do?" She looked at him then, squinted at him with one eye, and turned back to the sun. "But with the insurance settlements and his police benefits I can manage it."

"You know Miriam's going to hit the ceiling."

"I'm afraid I couldn't care less. She wants me to put him in a home up in Pittsburgh. It would be great for her—she could visit him every day, and I could only get there on weekends because of my job. She could keep on pretending that he's her little boy again. No thank you."

"There are some good places up in Pittsburgh."

"I think this will be better."

"I don't see how. . . ."

"You know what most nursing homes are like. How well are they going to take care of him? He just lies there, he can't tell anybody what he wants or needs. He'll be fine during the days till I can get there. He's certainly not going anyplace."

"But. . . ."

"And what about physical therapy? Nobody's going to work with him like I do. The new place is close enough that I can get home at lunchtime. He needs that so his muscles don't deteriorate any more than they have, so if he wakes up—"

"Debbie, he's not going to wake up. The doctors said—"

"The doctors have said a lot of things, haven't they?"

She sat up straight and lowered her face from the sky; she didn't want to get burned, even a gossamery sun could do damage. The two of them sat a long time, not saying anything. Across the street the bells of Holy Innocents rang that it was one o'clock; she'd have to get back soon. A crow flew down the sky, calling distantly, a wavy black line that disappeared into the trees on the other side of the valley. At their feet a pigeon toy-walked along the gravel path, hesitated, gave them a one-sided once-over, pecked at a pebble by mistake or from frustration, and toy-walked away. She put her hand to her forehead, a kind of salute, pretending to shield her eyes from a sky without glare. She wanted to get this over with.

"Dear Wally. Did you really think I was going to marry you or something?"

"Well, yeah, as a matter of fact I did. I thought that's what normally happens when people start sleeping together. And I told you I was going to leave my wife. . . ."

Dear sweet dumb Wally. "I couldn't do a thing like that as long as Ron's alive. I don't know if I ever could. You don't understand how special Ron and I were together. You don't find a love like ours every day. We were in tune with each other, we liked the same things and always knew what the other was thinking, we were perfect together—"

"That's the biggest bunch of bullshit I ever heard."

Debbie looked at him, blinked.

"Is that why he used to beat you up all the time? Is that your idea of a perfect love?"

She thought, So, you knew all along and you didn't do a thing to stop it. Why didn't you do something when I needed you? And she never spoke to Wally again. She got up from the bench and walked down the gravel path and out of the park, got in her car and drove back to the bank and that was that, he was out of her life.

Seven

It wasn't so much that she was angry with Wally, it was more that he simply ceased to exist for her. He was an absence, a hole in the air, a void exactly the size and shape of a love that was no more. Later, she would remember the times she spent with Wally as a special treasure, a jewel compared to the times she spent with other men—guys in bars or guys she worked with, guys she met at a friend's house or on vacation, always one-nighters, never any repeats—times she spent in order to survive. But if she happened to see Wally around town, if he came into the bank or if she ran into him at the supermarket, she dismissed him as if she had seen something dredged up from the currents or caverns of her undermind. She told herself that there was nobody there, told herself she was only being silly; she might lament Wally for a lifetime, but there was no changing her mind that he was gone.

But there was no time for sorrow, not at the present at any rate; there was too much else going on in her life, too many good things happening. She felt her life was changing and she had a new sense of purpose, she didn't want to squander her good feelings on anything that depressed her. She went ahead with her plans; and in another month she was settled in her new apartment on Orchard Hill, in a new building up Thirty-Seventh Street Extension in North Sheffield, a short distance from the hospital.

On Ron's moving day, everyone was particularly nice to Debbie. A day nurse was there to help the medics get Ron into the new hospital bed and make sure the IVs and the catheter and the monitors were hooked up correctly, as well as get all the other medical supplies unpacked and organized. It was nearly five thirty before Debbie had a chance to be alone with her husband, about the time she would usually get home from work.

After walking through the apartment once more to make sure everything was in order, she went back to the living room and stood for a moment at the balcony doors. It was dark on the late winter evening, the sky cobalt blue above darker raggedy Western Pennsylvania hills. Across the river, on the steep bluffs of the valley wall, an unseen truck was dumping molten slag down the hillside, the white-hot flow like the eruption of a small volcano. Farther down the valley, the slit in the earth that marked the town, was the glow of the business district, the lights of the mills along the river. She pulled the drapes closed and went over to her husband.

She checked the monitors, adjusted the drip of the IV. She buzzed his head up after mistakenly buzzing his head down.

"Oops, sorry sweetheart," she said and giggled to herself. "I'll have to get used to the controls."

He lay with his head slightly elevated, eyes closed, totally at peace, breathing regularly, barely noticeably. When the room was dark like this, and especially since she'd let his mustache grow bushy, he even looked like Ron at times; she thought she'd let his hair grow too, she was beginning to think that long hair on guys looked sexy. She smiled to him, then took off her skirt and shoes and blouse, her half-slip and bra and pantyhose; she was going to leave her panties on but thought he might like it better without so she took them off too. She climbed in the bed beside him, scrunching him over a little to give herself room and curling up against him. She spoke gently into the side of his impassive face.

"Here we are, sweetheart. Oh it's so good to have you back home again. I missed you so much. Oh, let me tell you what happened at work the other day. . . ."

. . . And it is all very clear to him. It is such a relief, not to be afraid of it anymore. It is simply here, in front of him. It doesn't matter the consequences. It is here. There's nothing now but to fulfill it.

Duncan rushes forward before the Indian can make any more of a cut into Hugh's scalp. His broadsword in his hand, screaming, "Tullochard!" The Indian stops, barely has time to look up at him, completely puzzled. Duncan's blade strikes him first down across his face, slicing it diagonally. As the Indian tries to spring backward, Duncan slices him again. And again and again, more times than necessary. Then he's on his knees beside Hugh. He rolls him over carefully onto his back and cradles Hugh's head in his lap. Pulls out his own shirttail and rips a strip of cloth from it and binds the cut on Hugh's head, the whole time crooning to him, "Oh laddie, oh laddie. . . ."

Hugh opens his eyes. "The Indian, he's . . ."

"I got him, he's dead. Hugh, I didna see him before, I didna understand. . . ."

"Och, it's all right, it's all right," Hugh pats his arm. "But you have to go. Leave me. . . ."

Duncan ignores him. He opens Hugh's jacket and finds the gunshot wound under his arm. It looks clean, maybe it didn't hit anything vital inside. He cuts Hugh free of the jacket and blood-soaked shirt and rips the rest of his own shirt and binds the wound the best he can. "You're lucky, Campbell, I'm such a bad shot."

Hugh laughs a little, more like a cough. He pats Duncan's arm. "I'm afraid, Dunnie my treasure. I'm afraid. . . ."

"You should be. All the way out here in the wilderness, with no but a Kenzie lad and some wee sheep to look out for you. But we'll do our best."

"That's no it—" Hugh breaks off, coughing.

"Save your strength, Campbell. You always did talk too much."

"Leave me . . ."

"Aye. So the crows can get you. They'd have one bite of you and you'd make them sick at their stomachs. Besides that, if I left you here the doxies at Fort Pitt would never forgive me. So, here we go then."

He lays their muskets on Hugh's chest, finds Hugh's grenadier hat and puts it there too, and wraps him in his plaid. Then Duncan squats and lifts the wounded man in his arms, gets him standing upright, then bends forward and lifts the man across his shoulders like a yoke. He rises slowly, getting the feel of the load.

"You'll no make it," Hugh whispers. "I'm too heavy."

"You're no sack of feathers and that's the way of it. But I've carried deer and a year-old calf and sheep this way before, and I guess I can carry a grenadier corporal too. You just make sure your pretty hair does no fall off before we get you there."

"Dunnie. . . ."

"Hush now."

Duncan sets his load again, looks around to make sure which way he needs to go, and starts back to the tree line. He staggers a little, then feels sure of the load. The sheep in the pen of branches watch the two men start to leave, milling around, wheeling in against each other. Then one, tentatively, breaks free of the others and starts to follow after the men. The others follow, scamper one after the other, in single file, to catch up. The little procession enters the trees, the one man carrying the other on his shoulders, the straggly line of sheep, heading back across the slope of the valley again. Looking for the way back.

HOLDING ON

1983

Robbie's chair was shaky, he felt as if he was about to tip over. He wiggled from side to side, trying to get settled, trying to find an even spot.

"You got ants?" Tom said.

"Chair's crooked." Robbie got up to move the aluminum chair to another spot but it was lighter than he anticipated; the chair jumped out of his grasp and landed a few feet away on its front legs and collapsed, folded in upon itself on the ground.

"You sure know how to fix things, Rob," Gary said.

"You'd think a foreman would have a better handle on things, wouldn't you?" Tom said, an edge to his voice.

Both Robbie and Gary looked at Tom to see where that was coming from. Robbie picked up the chair and hashed around in the grass in his backyard to find a level spot.

"When you get through," Tom said, "how about showing me the second-best spot?"

Robbie nodded as he sat again, made a comic face. Gave Tom the benefit of the doubt that the other was making a joke, hoped the bad moment had passed.

"House is looking good," Gary said. He lay stretched out on his chopper, his long lanky frame facing backward, elbows braced on the handlebars, being careful not to shift his weight and drive the kickstand further into the ground. "Painting's a lot of work."

"Next time I'm paying somebody to paint it," Robbie said.

"Next time you can afford to," Tom said. "Now that you're foreman." When Gary gave him a look, he added, "I'm just saying."

Robbie shook his head at Gary: Let it go. He found his chair was still shaky.

They heard it before they saw it. The minicycle came up the alley, the boy riding it revving the small 80cc engine when he saw the adults; Little Robbie turned into the yard and came rolling across the grass, past Gary stretched out on his cycle to where the other two men were sitting, placing the front wheel of the machine against the edge of the chair between Robbie's legs. The engine, even when idling, crackled and sputtered. The boy's head was encased in a bright orange helmet. Robbie looked at his son but all he could see in the black wraparound visor was a distorted image of himself.

"How's it running now?" he shouted to the boy.

Little Robbie shrugged. "It still cuts out on the low end." Coming from inside the helmet his son's voice sounded hollow and faraway.

"Your dad's good at fixing things," Tom said, loud enough for the others to hear but not necessarily the boy.

"Easy, son," Gary said, not to the boy. He took a long pull on his Rolling Rock, then unfolded himself from the back of the cycle. "Oof! Getting too old for this biker stuff. Think I'll trade it in on a nice comfortable see-dan."

"That'll be the day," Robbie said.

"When I die," Tom sang, finishing the Buddy Holly lyric.

"Bring it over here," Gary said, motioning to the boy. "Let me take a look at it, see if we can find out what's troubling this thing. Hoss, you got your tools handy?"

"They're in the back of my pickup," Robbie said, nodding to his truck parked on the edge of the grass.

Gary nodded and went over and got the toolbox out of the bed of the truck. Little Robbie walked the sputtering bike over to him and Gary squatted down and began tinkering.

After a few minutes, Little Robbie crackled off for another turn around the neighborhood. Gary put the toolbox back in Robbie's truck and came back across the grass; he crunched his empty beer can in his hand and took another from the cooler near the feet of the two men. He leaned his butt against the seat of the bike as he snapped open the can. "So, did Robbie tell you what you wanted to hear while I was away?"

"About what?" Tom said.

"Yeah, about what?" Gary said.

"You mean I can't just stop by my foreman's house for a friendly chat?" Tom said.

Robbie and Gary looked at each other, shook their heads at each other. Neither one buying it.

"I don't know any more about the mill closing than what I told you at work," Robbie said.

"They're not going to close the mill," Tom said, looking from one to the other. "That's all just a bunch of talk to scare us. This mill ain't going nowhere, just take a look at it, how're they going to walk away from a place like that? But I wouldn't be surprised if they're thinking layoffs."

"What he's getting at is," Gary said, "are you going to keep him on the crew."

I know what he's getting at, Robbie thought.

"So what's so wrong about that?" Tom said. Spreading his hands as if his intention was laid out there for all to see.

"Robbie'll take care of us, the best he can," Gary said, gazing up at the sky the color of lead above the valley.

"Yeah," Tom said. "He'll take care of you maybe, because you guys have worked together a long time. I want to know what happens to the rest of the crew."

Gary raised up slowly, stood beside his bike, leveled his gaze at Tom. "That's way out of line, son."

"Yeah, we'll see about that," Tom said, getting up from the chair. But he turned and walked away, back across the yard.

Robbie looked at Gary, shrugged, and decided he should be the proper host and walk him out. Tom headed between the houses, toward his Trans Am parked out front, Robbie trailing a dozen steps behind. As he started to get in, Tom called over the roof of the car without looking at him, "Thanks for the beer, Robbie."

"Yeah, anytime," Robbie called. But Tom was starting the car, sped away, down the street. Robbie had a moment's panic, wondering where Little Robbie was on his minicycle, but Tom made it to the corner and turned down the hill, mufflers racking off against the pull of gravity, then was gone, and Robbie could hear the minicycle somewhere in the distance behind him. As Robbie came back between the houses, Grace was standing on the back porch.

"I don't want him ripping around everywhere on that thing, Robbie. He'll disturb the whole neighborhood. That was our agreement, he'd only ride it on a track. . . ."

"I want him to give it a good trial while Gary's here to make any adjustments."

"Who was that other guy who just left? Is he part of your crew too? I thought Gary was bad enough. The three of you looked like hoodlums sitting out there, the neighbors'll think we're running a biker bar or something."

"The neighbors can think what they want."

"Well, does Gary have to park that old motorcycle right out there where everyone can see it?"

Robbie tried to laugh it away. "He brought it over to show me how he's restored it. We used to ride choppers like that back—"

"Yes, but you don't anymore. And don't get ideas of having those things around again. I've tried to make us a nice respectable home here. . . ."

"Leave it, Grace," Robbie said turning away, heading back across the yard. "Just leave it alone."

Gary had taken over Tom's vacant chair. When Robbie plopped down beside him, Gary said, "A little domestic dispute with Grace?"

Robbie shrugged it off. "It's called marriage."

"Sorry about Tom turning up, he must have heard us talking about me coming over today."

"It's okay. We're all concerned about what's going to happen."

"He still had no right bringing up that kind of shit. He and I are going to have us a little chat one of these days." Gary finished the beer and hoisted himself up out of the chair. "Guess I better get going. It sounds like Little Robbie's machine is running okay."

"If it weren't I'm sure he'd be back by this time," Robbie said, following his friend. "I appreciate you bringing over the bike."

"Yeah, I wanted you to see it. And I knew you'd never make it over to my place." As Robbie started to explain, Gary waved it away. The two men stood looking at the chopper. "You want to take it for a spin?"

Robbie started to say that he better not, then said, "Yeah. You mind?"

"Nah, course not. Thought you might."

Robbie straddled the bike, looked at Gary and grinned. He jumped on the kickstarter a couple of times but nothing happened. He reached down to make sure the gas tank was open—it

wasn't, the cock was closed, dumb Robbie—and this time the
engine caught.

"Careful letting it out," Gary shouted to him over the crackling of the straight pipes. "It's a deadman clutch, just like the
original."

Robbie gunned the engine and tried to anticipate the clutch,
but its grab was total and quick: the bike shot forward a couple
of feet, the front wheel lifting off the ground, until it stalled.

"Whoa, hoss!"

"Told ya. It's brutal. You want me to take it?"

At the end of the alley, he saw Little Robbie coming down the
street toward them on the minicycle, riding slowly, standing on
the pegs, revving the engine, the black visor up, his face all smiles,
proud of himself.

"I've got it," Robbie said.

Robbie jumped on the starter and fired it up again. Again he
raced the throttle a couple of times and tried to anticipate the
clutch, but the lurch forward surprised him a second time and
the front wheel lifted again, only this time the acceleration threw
him back, Robbie twisting the throttle open even further until
the bike was upright, standing on its rear wheel, engine racing,
sloughing him off the back end, and still he held on to the grips.

"Let it go! Let it go!" he remembered Gary yelling at him.

But he wouldn't let go, not as the bike went faster, not as he
started to run with it, or was towed along by it, for a brief second
looking as if he were dancing with the upright machine, engaged
in a deadly footrace with the bike standing as tall as he was; he
did not let go even as he felt the bone of his right leg shatter
down into his ankle, like stubbing the end of a two-by-four with
a sledge hammer; he only released his hold on the grips when he
managed to pull the standing motorcycle backward, pull it over
and steer-wrestle it to the ground, on top of himself, Robbie collapsing under it but at least stopping the machine, saving it,

keeping it from running away, the rear wheel of the overturned cycle on its side now spinning furiously into the loose tar and gravel of the alley and then digging into his pinned body as the engine went crazy and he went crazy finally with the pain.

Acknowledgments

There are four people—friends, actually; dream catchers—without whom I could never have brought these books to publication:

Barbara Clark
Kim Francis
Dave Meek
Jack Ritchie

I also thank Eileen Chetti for struggling through my quirks of style and punctuation; Linnea Duly for writing a study guide; Bob Gelston, who is always around to answer questions and take on anything else that's needed. And then, of course, there's my wife Marty. . . .

Portions of this book were written during a fellowship from the Pennsylvania Council on the Arts. Some of the stories in this collection have appeared, sometimes in different form, in the following magazines: "Larry-Berry" and "Holding On" (published as "Down in the Greenwood O"), *New England Review and Bread Loaf Quarterly;* "Making Do" (published as "Back to Lovelock"), *California Quarterly.*

Richard Snodgrass lives in Pittsburgh, PA with his wife Marty and two indomitable female tuxedo cats, raised from feral kittens, named Frankie and Becca.

To read more about the Furnass series, the town of Furnass, and special features for *Holding On*—including a Reader's Study Guide, author interviews, and omitted scenes—go to www.RichardSnodgrass.com.